LOVING SOLOMONS ISLAND

A Chesapeake Bay Romance Series

C.A. Burkhart

IBSN: 9798335395427

Cover design by: C.A. Burkhart
Library of Congress Control Number: 2018675309
Printed in the United States of America

For all my Maryland Girlies <3

CONTENTS

CONTENT WARNING

Loving Solomons Island contains depictions of domestic violence, including physical, emotional, and psychological abuse. The content may be distressing or triggering for some readers. Please proceed with caution and prioritize your well-being. If you or someone you know is affected by domestic violence, support resources are available.

National Domestic Violence Hotline- 1(800)-799-7233
RAINN Hotline- 1(800)-656-4673

1

Ryder

I get off my plane quickly and search for the nearest bathroom.

Holding it in for the four-hour flight while having a whiskey coke was not one of my brightest ideas, but the bathrooms on planes are far too confined for my liking.

The terminal is busy, but I see the sign for the bathroom and push my way past the slow walkers. I'm nearly busting, slinging my work bag over my shoulder as I fuddle with my zipper. It finally gave, and I started to relieve myself until my cell phone rang.

"Fuck!" I turned my wrist to see who was calling from my smartwatch. My boss's name flashes across its screen. I groaned and touched my headset to answer the call, "Hello?"

"Ryder, my boy! Did you make it to Baltimore?" Dave all but screamed through the phone. He's old and thinks the louder you speak, the better someone can hear you on the phone, but he sounds like an idiot most of the time. I laid my head against my hand, which rested on the wall behind the urinal to help elevate some of the pain I was going through, holding back the lake that now resides in my bladder.

"Yes, just landed." I tried to make my words less strained but quickly lost the battle.

"Good! The car is at baggage claim to pick you up and take you to your new home for the next eight weeks, Solomons Island, Maryland. It's an hour and a half drive from the airport. Your home away from home will be on C Street in the heart of the town, and I know of a fantastic local bar called Sunset Escape that's within walking distance! And if I know you, you'll be spending a pretty penny on the company's credit card there!" He let out a hardy laugh.

I huffed, "Thanks for the info. I have to go, Dave. I'll call you in the morning." I didn't give him time to say goodbye before I hung up and immediately relieved myself. "Holy shit. I think I see stars." I finished my business in the bathroom and headed to baggage claim.

I saw my bag on the carousel, grabbed it, and walked over to the transportation bay. I see a man in a suit holding a sign with my name. I raise my hand, waving, "Hi, I'm Ryder Reed."

"Good evening, Mr. Reed. I am your driver for this trip. Right this way, sir."

I followed him to an all-blacked-out escalade, hopped in the back, and soon we were on the road to my next destination.

I checked the time on my watch, and the screen said eight in the evening. Classical music began playing throughout the car, and my eyes started to feel heavy.

A quick nap won't hurt, Ryder.

I adjusted in the seat, leaning against the window, and let the Beethoven-esque music lull me to sleep.

2

Clover

"Shit, shit, shit, shit, shit, shit! I'm going to be late! Aunt Diana is going to kill me! It's the first day of summer, and I know Sunset will be packed!" I smudged deep red lipstick on my lips in the mirror by the front door, quickly shoved the tube in my purse, and slipped on my work shoes. I did my triple-tap reminder before I left my house, "Bra, check!" I said as I cupped my securely padded breasts. "Phone, check!" I touched the back pocket of my jeans, where my phone mostly lives. "And lastly, keys!" I shook my purse and heard the familiar jingle of my keys. "Great. Now I have to run to work." I checked my watch. "It takes ten minutes to get there, and I have exactly...ten minutes before my shift. Time to put your new running shoes to good use, Clover." I said, trying to hype myself up.

I locked the door behind me and sprinted down the street when I saw a shiny new escalade pull into the driveway of the vacation house down the street. "Great, new loud neighbors for a week. Just what I needed." I huffed and set off down the road for my shift at Sunset.

◆ ◆ ◆

"Clover Langley, You are late again!" Aunt Diana yelled from the other end of the sand pit bar.

"I know! I know! I'm so sorry. The lookOut was so busy tonight, and they needed help in the kitchen, and well, here I am." I gave her a look of innocence.

"You're lucky you're my niece, and I own this bar. Get to work. And go tell Rory we are out of ice over here!" She shouts as I make my way over to the employee room.

I entered the small room, hanging my purse and sweater in the slim locker with my name on it, and tied my curly red hair in a bun, pulling a few pieces around my face. I walked over to the sink in the room and washed my hands. The small mirror that hangs above it has a big crack in it from when an old employee brought her jealous boyfriend to work, and he tried to beat up my Uncle Rory. He must have been new around here because everyone from here knows how in love my Uncle Rory is with my Aunt Diana. It's almost sickening how lovey-dovey they are with each other. He kisses the ground she walks on, and I'm so *jealous*. I stand on my tippy toes to look over the crack. My freckled face and green eyes have landed me nothing but losers. The last one being the *ultimate* loser. I touched the high point of my cheek around my eye, which was black and blue over a year ago. Somehow, the skin still feels tender, or it might just be the memories.

Jason Hunt was a smooth talker. He liked to flirt with all the girls, and when it was my turn, I was no better than the rest. I fell into his charms and got too swept up to notice the red flags. His drinking became worse, and he came home from the bar one night out of his mind, and he hit me. It only took that one time for me to know that if I didn't leave, I was never going to, so I did. I kicked him out of the house we bought together on C Street and moved my three best friends, Rain, Iris, and Aiden, in.

We have all been friends since childhood, and living with them has been the most incredible breath of fresh air. No more walking on eggshells or breathing the wrong way. I let out a sad laugh. I still have a lot of healing to do.

I finished up in the employee room and went to find Uncle Rory before Aunt Diana wrung my neck.

3

Ryder

I unpacked all my clothes and toiletries, and by the time I was done, the crab-shaped clock on the wall in my new 'home away from home' said ten thirty. My stomach growled as I took out my phone to search if that bar Dave mentioned was still open. "I know. I know." I said, trying to hush the growing growl. "I didn't eat at the airport, and I should have, but no worries, the bar is still open." I placed my phone in my pocket and set off on the fifteen-minute walk to the bar, seeing as I didn't have a vehicle yet.

I researched the island before coming to Solomons Island, where a boardwalk runs half a mile down the Chesapeake Bay. However, Solomons Island is only a mile and a half long and not technically an island. It's attached to the mainland by one road that loops around the mile-and-a-half stretch of land, making it more secluded. Most of the restaurants along the strip on the boardwalk have good reviews, and the town is community-centered, with events almost every weekend from spring until late fall.

My boss, Dave, and his corporate executive buddies vacationed here last summer. They all thought this place could use a shopping center, so they sent me, the company's best land procurement manager, to scope out the best plot of land and strike a deal with the owners of said properties on behalf of the company.

I'm the middleman.

I'm so sick of being the middleman.

I ran my fingers through my hair, interlocking my fingers behind my neck. I used to love it over ten years ago when I was still young, but I'm thirty-five now, and I would like to settle down in one place and stay there, maybe meet someone and start a family. But I can't do that if I'm always moving around. I haven't stayed in any place longer than six months in my entire life. Everything I own fits in a single suitcase. Growing up in the foster system prepared me for this life, I guess. At least it's an upgrade from where everything used to be stored in black trash bags.

I could hear the bar before seeing it, and it lived up to its name. It's beach-themed, with several sizable fake island tiki heads out front—'Sunset Escape,' the sign reads.

Once you enter, you see tiki-head stools that line the indoor bar, and the further you walk into the bar, the more it opens to the outside. An open-area sand pit greets you, and a stage is at the back. Two bars on either side lead up to the stage, each packed with patrons. I wait a moment to see if the crowd clears as people gather on the stage with instruments, piquing the interest of several bargoers.

I turned my attention back to see if I could sit at the bar now that the crowd was clearing, and that's when I saw the most gorgeous woman I had ever seen.

Her hair is in a bun with ringlets of red curls that fall around her sweet, round face. She laughs at something one of the patrons says, and it's like a song I have been dying to hear.

I sit at the bar, and she smiles, "Hi! What can I get ya?" She asked.

It takes me a moment to remember how words work. "Hi, uh, can I get a menu? Do you serve food here?"

"Yeah! The kitchen closes in forty minutes, so pick what you want quickly. Chef doesn't like to be kept late." She says as she hands me a laminated menu, "We are out of rockfish tonight."

"Thank you." I looked over the menu and saw various seafood options mixed with classic American dishes.

"I recommend the crab cake bites. They are my favorite." She said with that same breathtaking smile.

"I will have that then. Thank you for the recommendation." I smiled, handing back the menu back.

"I'll get that in and be right back to get your drink order." She bit her lip slightly, sending a tingle down my spine.

"I'll be waiting," I said, giving her a wink.

She disappeared behind a beaded curtain in what I can assume is the kitchen. I turned to watch the band play and quickly concluded that their music was best played for deaf ears, or in this case, the heavily intoxicated.

"So what can I get ya to drink?" I turned to face the redheaded goddess. She's leaning against the bar, and I can see her features more clearly now. She has green eyes and freckles that cover every visible part of her pale skin. My guess is she's covered in them head-to-toe. My mind sends me downright dirty thoughts, and I push those quickly away.

"Whiskey coke, please."

"Coming right up."

4

Clover

He has to be the hottest man I have ever seen. I can't keep my thoughts or eyes from wandering from the man sitting at my bar's end. From what I could tell, he was at least six feet tall when I saw him walking over to the bar. He has medium-length jet-black hair that tapers in on the sides and looks like he jumped out of a K-pop music video.

Sexy sweat and all.

I watched as he sipped his whiskey coke until I heard the Chef call an order up. I returned to the kitchen, grabbed the order of the crab cake bites, and brought them out to this stranger who captivated me. I smiled, handing him the food basket, "Here you go! Do you need anything else?" Maybe, me, perhaps? No, Clover. You don't need that right now, plus he's a literal stranger.

"What's your name?" He asked.

A blush rises to my cheeks, "Clover Langley. What's yours?"

"Ryder Reed. It's a pleasure to meet you, Clover." He held out his hand for me to shake, and when I grabbed it, my hand went tingly all over.

I took my hand back, ignoring the feeling, "Where are you from, Ryder Reed?"

"Do I not look like I'm from here?" He joked.

I laughed, shaking my head, "Unfortunately, I know everyone in this town and would have remembered you." He smirks, and I'm sure my cheeks are crimson now. I shouldn't be flirting with him, but something about him keeps drawing me back. I don't need a relationship. I've sworn off dating after everything ended with Jason, but what harm can flirting do? Right?

"I'm from nowhere and everywhere all at once, but I grew up in Houston, for the most part," Ryder said.

"Oh, we got ourselves a Texan here! What brings you to the East Coast and little old Solomons Island?" I asked.

"Business. Boring, boring business." He laughed, taking a bite of one of the three crab cakes, and moaned, his eyes rolling to the back of his head. His deep voice sent a heatwave to my core, and I bit my lip. "I see why these are your favorite. This is fantastic. Thank you."

"I'm happy you like them." I smiled until I saw Robby Dasher coming up in my peripheral.

Great.

"Hey, Clo. What's going on over here?" Robby asked in an accusatory tone.

"I'm serving my customers, Robby. Would you like anything?" I bit back, annoyed.

"Nah. I'm good. Rory's got me covered. It was good seeing you, Clo. I'll tell Jason you said hi." I swallowed hard, and Robby returned to the band, joining the drunken crowd.

"Excuse me for a moment," I say without making eye contact with Ryder.

I entered the kitchen and closed myself in the walk-in freezer. I felt the tears welling up and tried everything to stop them. I breathed deeply, gently wiping at my bottom lashes to prevent the tears from falling. Using what I learned from therapy, I grounded myself, breathing in and out, taking a moment to remember how far I've come in the last year and how far I will go because I will never let myself be that vulnerable again. I wiped the last of the tears away and returned to the bar.

Ryder is still sitting at the bar with a worried look. "Sorry, I needed to go check on something in the freezer. The kitchen is also closed for the evening, meaning this bar will close for the night. You can still sit at the tables in the middle of the bar on the other side, but the indoor bar and kitchen are closed. Last call is in twenty minutes, so I'd do that now if you want another Whiskey coke." I smiled shyly, "It was nice to meet you, Ryder Reed. Good luck with your boring business trip."

He holds his hand for a handshake, and I hesitate before I slide my hand into his. His touch felt electric against my skin this time, and I wondered how it would feel to have his hands on my body. Would it feel the same?

Jesus, Clover, get a grip!

"The pleasure was mine, Clover Langley." The way Ryder said my name made my knees weak.

The grip is so far from my grasp.

I watched as he got up and sat at a table near the bar, mostly watching me clean up rather than the live music. I cleaned the bar quickly to free myself from his gaze, which made me incredibly flustered. I stopped by the employee room to say goodnight to Aunt Diana, grabbed my things from my locker, and headed home.

5

Ryder

The next day passed rather quickly as I looked over the town's blueprints, mapping out where we could and could not build, but my mind wandered all day, thinking back to the redhead from the bar last night.

Clover.

Her name bounced around my head all day, and I decided to see if she was working at the bar tonight. If she's not there, I will grab an order of the crab cake bites to go.

Clover hasn't been the only thing I've been dreaming about.

My rental car was dropped off in the afternoon, and I wanted to take it for a test drive before I headed to the bar. I've had a long day hunched over a map and computer screen and needed to leave this godforsaken beach-themed house.

I wouldn't mind if it were a soft beach theme, but this house gives, 'Look at me! Tourist visit here!' vibes. It was like a Tommy Bahama threw up here. Needless to say, the house was giving me a headache.

I locked the front door behind me and turned to approach the shiny new Volkswagen Atlas Cross Sport.

"Damn, Dave. You outdid yourself this time." He usually set me up in a good rental car, but this is fancy even for him. He must really want this deal.

I looked across the street before getting into the car to see Clover standing in a driveway, talking to a man and woman a few yards away. Unlike when Robby interrupted us last night, she seemed happy talking to them. It took everything in me not to beat his smug little face and whoever Jason was.

"Bye! I'll see you guys tonight." She said, waving them off, walking down the street, and headed toward the bar.

I quickly got into my car and rushed after her, catching her just before she turned onto the main road. I rolled down my passenger window. "Miss Clover Langley, it's lovely to see you again." She looked around, fear written on her face, which set off my primal urge to protect her. Something or someone is scaring her. "Clover, are you alright?"

"Now is not a good time. I'm kind of in a rush," she said, her eyes still darting around, looking at the parked cars over at the boardwalk across the street.

"I can give you a ride. I was just going out to test drive the new rental my company dropped off for me." She looked at the cars again, and I finally saw who she saw.

Robby from last night, some blonde douchebag next to him, and several other douchebag look-a-likes hanging around three tricked-out Jeeps. The blonde one was staring at us while Robby was speaking to him. "Get in the car, Clover. You're late already, and it's my fault. Let me make it right." Clover hesitates but agrees, and she opens the door and steps into my car.

Her fresh flower-scented perfume was the first thing that hit me, and I took a deep breath, inhaling her divine scent, closing my eyes, and committing it to memory. When I open them again, I'm looking straight over at the blonde douchebag. I gave him a smirk and pulled away.

"So, where to?" I asked.

"The LookOut. It's right up here on the left." I nod, knowing exactly where it's at after looking at maps of this town today. I pulled into the restaurant parking lot and found a spot close to the front. "Thank you so much for the ride. That was kind of you." she fuddled with her hands in her lap.

"Repayment for recommending the crab cake bites to me. I have dreamt about them all day, among other–things." Her cheeks blush, and the color that spreads over her face makes her green eyes pop.

I wanted to make her blush like that all the time.

"I'm glad you liked them. I'll be working over there later tonight. I get off here at nine and then head to Sunset until eleven thirty... And I'm telling a stranger my entire work schedule, so please don't be a murderer. That would suck." She said in a defeated tone.

I laughed, "I am not a murderer. I just travel for work. I promise."

Clover laughed with me, "Good. As I said, that would suck, at least for me." We locked eyes briefly, and my heartbeat jumped up to my throat. "I'm sorry for Robby last night. He's just a jerk. The rest of the patrons aren't like him. It's fun at Sunset, usually."

"You don't need to apologize for him. He can do that himself, but I feel I won't get one, and that's okay. But don't you dare apologize for him." She nodded, giving me a shy smile.

"Here," she pulled a pen from her apron and grabbed my hand. "Here's my number. Text me sometime?" Her green eyes sparkled as she spoke.

"I will."

Clover hopped out of my car and headed into the restaurant. The feel of her hands against mine made me curious to know her more. I know she felt something, too.

I drive out of the parking lot, passing the douche parade once again on my way out.

6

Clover

My shift at the LookOut runs over, as usual, these days, but at least I brought a change of clothes with me this time.

Running back to the house would *not* be ideal today.

Robby ran to Jason last night and told him I was 'eye fucking' a customer, and he has been blowing up my phone ever since from private numbers. But *seeing* Jason parked at the boardwalk today freaked me the fuck out. I haven't seen him in a year because his rich daddy shipped him off to rehab in another state, and the last I heard, he found god and a girl out there and planned to stay wherever he was sent. I didn't think he would return here after his actions, but I'm proven wrong about him once again.

I changed my clothes in the employee bathroom, tip out for the night, and told the kitchen staff goodnight before leaving. I reach into my back pocket, pulling out my phone, when it vibrates in my hand. I open my phone, and a message from an unknown number pops up on the screen, "I'm outside waiting to take you to Sunset. :) -Ryder"

My heart fluttered, and the butterflies I once knew returned to my stomach. It's been so long since someone made me feel this way, and it scares me, but at least now I'm not that naive girl I once was, and I won't be making the same mistakes.

I made my way to the Volkswagen and knocked on the window. The door unlocked, and I opened it. "You didn't have to pick me up. I could have walked," I said, smiling, not hiding my happiness that he was here.

"I wanted to ensure you got there safe, plus the crab cake bites, remember?" I laughed, getting into the car, and Ryder smiled. He was too good-looking to be flirting with me like this. "I also wanted to ask you on a date, if you're not too busy this weekend?" Ryder asked, and the butterflies started to stir once again.

"I just happen to be free tomorrow, which is rare for a Saturday, but I think I could squeeze you in somewhere." I realized the double meaning of my words before I could stop myself from saying it. "I, well, that's not what I meant. Of course, I would love to." I laughed nervously.

We pulled up in front of Sunset, but Ryder stopped me before I could get out and made me wait for him to open my door. He's such a gentleman, and it's making me rethink my stance on relationships. That is until I saw the Jeeps over in the side parking lot, making my heart drop. I stumbled out of the car as Ryder opened the door, but thankfully, Ryder's hand was already outstretched for me to take, and he saved me from eating the pavement. "Sorry! I wasn't paying attention," I said, looking up at him.

"No need to apologize, Clover." His deep voice skated across my skin, sending goosebumps everywhere. I was so close to him that I couldn't help breathing him in.

God, he smells like what I imagine a Greek god to smell like smoky embers, with a hint of sandalwood. I straightened myself, trying to steady my heart rate. "Would you like to come in? Wait, you already told me you were, sorry, I mean–"

"Come on, Clover." He held out his arm for me to take, so I wrapped my arm around his. I stare up at him, taking him in, and my heart again beats out of rhythm just by how he looks back at me.

We walked inside Sunset, and it was crazy busy tonight with a new local band playing, and it's the start of the first weekend in summer. I'm usually busy on Friday nights, but it looks slammed. I let go of Ryder's arm and pulled his face down to my level so he could hear me, "I've gotta go. Enjoy your night. I'll see you tomorrow." I smiled, and then he picked up my hand, kissing my knuckles, and I swear my knees buckled just a little bit.

"I'll pick you up and take you home. Have a good shift." He smiled, and before I could object, he walked over to the take-out counter, grabbed a bag, and waved goodbye.

◆ ◆ ◆

It was midnight before I finished all my clean-up duties to prepare for the weekend. Aunt Diana and Uncle Rory had already left because it was my turn to close up shop. Chef left five minutes ago, so I hurried to my locker, grabbed my purse, took out my keys, and locked up on my way out.

The night went by in a blur, and I didn't see Jason at all despite his Jeep being here when I arrived. He kept his distance, or one of his little buddies used his Jeep.

I looked around the front parking lot to find Ryder, but it was empty. I walked to the parking lot, where I found Jason making out with a girl against his Jeep.

Great. Just when I thought I was in the clear.

I backed out of the street lamp that lit the side parking lot, hoping he wouldn't see me as I tried to hide in the dark. I was almost in the clear if it wasn't for the stupid rat that ran across my foot, sending me stumbling back into the light.

"Hey! Clo! Come meet my new girlfriend, Gina!" Jason yelled.

I sighed, turning to face him. "No thanks, Jason. I need to get home." He took a step forward, coming towards me, and I felt that deep fear in the pit of my stomach I felt over a year ago. "Don't come any closer to me, Jason Hunt. I may have made a deal with your daddy not to involve the cops, but that does not mean you can come anywhere near me. Stay away from me, Jason. I mean it."

That drunken glee her had before was wiped clean off his face, "Oh, so you think you're all big and tough now? A year away from me, and you've already moved on, Clo?"

"I moved on the moment your fist connected with my face, Jason." I bit out, "And I see you *haven't* changed in a year, still a drunk. I'm glad to see your daddy's money went to waste, ya know, with him sending you to rehab and all. Have a good night, Gina. Get home safe. Goodbye *forever*, Jason." I turned to find Ryder waiting a few feet away at the back of his car. I didn't turn back to see Jason's face as I walked over to Ryder, but I could sense he was as pissed as I imagined by the smile on Ryder's face. "I would like to leave immediately, and no, I don't want to talk about it." Ryder moves past me, opens the passenger door, and ensures I'm secure in my seat before closing the door. He quickly crosses over to his side, hops in the driver seat, and we take off toward my house, "I live on C street."

"I know," Ryder says.

I turned towards him, "How do you know where I live?" Fear jumped into my throat for a second time tonight as I realized that Ryder was still very much a stranger, and what he had just said set off all my alarm bells.

"I am staying at the vacation home across the street from your house. That's how I saw you this afternoon. I promise I'm not a creep, and I was going to test-drive the rental." He flashes a look of innocence.

I relaxed back into my seat. "Sorry, I'm just on edge and exhausted from a busy night."

"No, you were right to question me. Don't say sorry for being safe."

I smiled. The butterflies were at it again.

We pulled into the driveway of the vacation home, and I looked over at Ryder again, "I wanted to walk you home, as cheesy as it sounds, and maybe we can ask each other questions on the way there to get to know each other a little better before tomorrow?"

The butterflies were doing acrobats in my stomach right now, "Sure. I would like that." Ryder exited the car and crossed to my side, letting me out, "So who goes first?" I asked.

Ryder chuckled, "Ladies first, of course."

We started our slow stroll to my driveway, "How old are you?" I asked.

He smirked, "I'm thirty-five. How old are you?"

"I'm twenty-nine. When's your birthday?"

"The twelfth of April," Ryder said.

"Oooo! An Aries! No wonder you're so forward." We laughed.

"What about you? When's your birthday?" Ryder asked.

"November second. I'm a Scorpio. We are passionate and fiery despite being a water sign. We are also observant, and we *never* forget. Because Mars and Pluto rule our sign, we have a lot of general chaos in our daily lives, too." Ryder looks confused. "Do you know about astrology? I've been studying it on my own for years now."

"I have no idea what you're saying to me, but I know you look pretty while you do," Ryder said, flashing a smile.

My face flushes, and I smile shyly, tucking my hair behind my ear, "I could teach you about it if you'd like. People say it's just a bunch of crap, but the truth is the planets have more influence over our lives than we think."

"Oh, is that so?" Ryder asks.

I smile wide, "I hope so."

"And why's that?" He asks while taking a step closer to me.

I hadn't realized we were already in my driveway, with my back nearly against the garage door. He reached out, grabbing my hip, his touch feather-light. "Um, because–I—" He closed the distance between us, and his masculine scent again invaded my senses.

Ryder raised his other hand, cupping my face and angling it up to look him in the eyes. "You were saying?" He said with a smile that would break a thousand hearts.

"That um—the plants—planets, the planets have a heavy—influence a-and—" Ryder silences my rambling with a kiss. The kiss was soft, and I craved more. I reached up, placing my hands against his chest, and he felt like a solid rock beneath them. A soft moan escaped from our lips, and that's when Ryder pulled back, breaking our kiss. I'm left panting, wanting more, and his eyes said he wanted to do much more than kissing. "That's why everyone thinks Scorpios are a fire sign. We have all the other zodiac signs under our little spell."

"Call me bewitched then. You, Clover Langley, on the other hand, are entirely otherworldly. I will see you tomorrow. I'll pick you up at noon." Ryder said as he backed away slowly.

"I'll see you tomorrow, Ryder Reed." I watched him walk down the driveway and over to his place.

When he reached his door, I walked inside my house and was immediately bombarded by my best friends and roommates, Iris and Rain.

"Who the hell is that hottie?" Rain asked.

"I don't even like men and thought he was quite attractive." Iris chimes.

"Will you two let me get in the door? Please?" I asked, and they dispersed from the front door, no longer crowding me.

"Your Chinese food is in the microwave, ready for you to eat. I reheated it about five minutes ago." Iris said, flipping her long blonde hair over her shoulder.

Iris is the mother figure of our friend group, and we love her for it. She's the glue that keeps us together, but mostly me. She was there for me almost every day after I left Jason, helping me pick up the pieces of my shattered life.

"Thank you! I am starving." I walked to the microwave, took out my lukewarm leftovers, and ate. I looked up momentarily to see Iris and Rain gathered around the kitchen island. "What?" I asked with a mouth full of shrimp lo mein.

Rain leaned over the counter, her hands resting under her chin, and she gave me a doe-eyed look.

"You know what, Clover! Spill! Who was that *overly* attractive man that had you *cornered* against the garage, sucking your face?" Iris said.

My face heated, and they laughed. "Man, you got it bad. She doesn't stand a chance," Rain said as she put her thick brunette hair up into a bun.

Rain and Iris are as pretty as their names. Rain with her amber eyes and creamy pale skin with no freckle or blemish in sight.

Iris is a true blonde beauty with icy blue eyes and perfectly tanned skin from working at the local beaches as a lifeguard every summer since she was sixteen. "I met him last night at Sunset. His name is Ryder, and we have a date tomorrow." I admitted.

Iris gasped, "Shut up! A date! You haven't been on a date since—"

"Yes, thank you so much for reminding me, Iris. I saw Jason tonight." A collective gasp this time, "He was making out with some girl named Gina in the side parking lot. He asked me to come over to meet her."

"And what did you say?" Rain asked hesitantly.

"I told him no. He got upset and tried walking toward me, but I stopped him and told him exactly what I thought about him. Ryder was already there to pick me up and drove me home afterward. I didn't want to stick around after what I said."

"I bet that felt good," Iris said, grabbing my hand.

I laced my fingers with hers, "It did—It does—But if I'm being honest, I still have that small dark part of my brain that says, 'But what if he tries to hurt you again because of what you said.' I hate that because it still feels like he has some control over me."

Rain and Iris round the kitchen island and wrap their arms around me. "We love you and are so proud of how far you've come. It sucks he's back in town, but you're so much stronger than you were a year ago, Clover. Plus, I'm sure mister hottie across the street would be willing to be your bodyguard." Iris said, and I gave her a playful jab.

"I'm going to bed now. I'm exhausted, and I need to be well-rested for tomorrow. Thanks for trying to cheer me up, though. I love you guys," I said as I picked up my Chinese food to take to my room.

"Love you, babes!" Iris said.

"Ditto! Love you, babes! Goodnight!" Rain said, and I headed up the steps to my room.

7

Ryder

I checked myself out in the mirror for the thousandth time, ensuring my outfit didn't make me look entirely stupid. I was undecided but had no other options in my suitcase, so I wore my workout clothes. They have a more relaxed feel, my light gray shorts and black sleeveless shirt, but they fit what I had planned for my date with Clover today.

I looked at my smartwatch to check the time, and the screen said eleven forty-five. "Better early than late," I said, heading towards Clover's.

Her home and this neighborhood were rather lovely and upscale. The homes looked mostly like new builds or had been renovated to look like the newer builds to increase their property value. With three cars parked in the driveway of her home, I'm assuming she lives with roommates, but even with roommates, it still must be a pretty penny to rent in this neighborhood.

I raised my hand to knock on Clover's front door, but before my knuckles could meet the wooden door, it swung open, and there stood a petite blonde woman with her hand on her hip and a scowl on her face. "You're early, Mr. Garage Door Hottie. Give her five minutes. You can come in and sit in the living room. Watch out for Aiden—he bites," she said as she walked back into the house.

"Is Aiden your dog?" I asked, following the scary blonde woman to the living room.

"Aiden is a gay man with stud finders for teeth, and you,

my guy, are not safe. Although, he is sleeping currently, so you're good—for now." She smiled, sticking her hand out, "I'm Iris, by the way."

I shook her hand and was surprised by her firm handshake, "Ryder Reed or Mr. Garage Door Hottie is fine too."

She snickered, but her smile grew into a look of concern in the passing silence until Iris said, "Something is *different* about you. Clover needs different. But if you lay a finger on her, everyone in this house will 'goodbye earl' you, if you catch my drift. We love her very much, so please, don't break our girl. She's been repaired once already."

I felt my heart catch in my throat, and I wanted to ask more, but Clover came into view as she stood at the top of the steps, "You're early, Ryder. Thank you for being my guard dog, Iris."

My mouth nearly fell to the floor.

Clover had on, by all accounts 'normal clothes" with her loose-fit black Nirvana t-shirt and black biker shorts, but, *Holy fuck*, she's gorgeous. Her hair is in a messy bun with pieces perfectly framing her face, drawing my attention to her sweet-pea-green eyes. Her freckles looked so ethereal, and *my god*, was she curvy like a goddess, too. I wanted to sink my teeth into those hips of hers—a jab to the rib from scary Iris brought me back to reality. "You look beautiful, Clover." The blush that crept up on her cheeks pulled on my heartstrings.

"Thank you." Clover smiled, making me desperate to kiss her soft, full lips again. "Where are we going today?" she asked.

"It's a surprise, but there is no need to worry. I will give my number to Iris, and she can share it with your friends to track our location at all times. I would like to up my current reputation of Mr. Garage Door Hottie to Mr. *Safe* Garage Door Hottie," I said, giving them both a wink. Clover's broad smile spread to her friend Iris's face, but Iris quickly tried to hide it.

"Good. Safety is good." Iris said and handed me her phone. I sent myself a message on her phone and then took mine out to share my location with her.

"Shall we go then?" I asked Clover.

"Absolutely." She said, pulling her bag over her shoulder.

I held my hand for Clover to take, and she did. Her hand fit perfectly in mine, and her skin was so soft. Her softness made my hands want to search for more places to touch, but I would do this at her speed, if even at all. If what Iris alluded to is true, then I don't want to be someone who causes more grief for her. I will be what she needs me to be, even if I am just a friend.

I walked Clover to my car, opening the door for her, and as she got in, the scent of her perfume hit me. She smelled like summer rain with a hint of floral sweetness. It took all my strength not to bury myself in her neck. I don't know what's come over me, and I quickly shut the door and, rounding my side, hopped into the driver's seat and took off.

After a moment, Clover turned to me in her seat. "So, can I know now where you're taking me?" she asked.

I chuckled, "Don't like *not* being in control, do we, Clover Langley?"

She smirked, "You're right. It makes me nervous, but this is a good nervous."

I laughed harder this time, "I am very spontaneous, Clover. I have lived most of my life moving from place to place. I do things on a whim out of habit. Last month, I was staying in Pueblo, Colorado, and I drove to Albuquerque, New Mexico, because I saw a TikTok of a restaurant I wanted to try."

Clover laughed and relaxed in her seat. "You mentioned moving the other night. Were you a military kid? Growing up near a base, we always had new kids in school."

I took a deep breath and decided to tell her the truth. "I was a foster kid. A rebellious one that got kicked out of a lot of homes. I aged out of the foster system in Texas." This is where people usually feel sorry for me, but Clover—didn't.

Clover offered me her hand and said, "My parents were junkies. They were always looking for their next high instead of caring for me. They overdosed when I was ten, and I went to live with my Aunt Diana and Uncle Rory. Parents are overrated sometimes."

My heartstrings pulled again, and I squeezed her hand slightly while rubbing my thumb against the side of her hand, "Yes, they are."

I pulled into the New Carrollton Metro Garage, and Clover immediately asked, "Are we going to DC? I haven't been there in years. Are we going to a game? Is it football season? No, that's always around my birthday. Oh, wait, is it baseball? I'm not a fan, but we'll have fun."

I laughed, "It's not a sports outage. I despise sports, and going to a game of any kind sounds like torture. No more guessing, Clover—just enjoy the journey." Her cheeks flushed, and this time, I couldn't help myself. I cupped her face and leaned in close, "Let's have some fun, Clover." Her lips hovered close to mine, and all it would take would be one of us leaning in to seal them together. But I don't, and she pulled back a bit, "The train should be here soon." I said, and Clover nods.

I get out, rounding her side, and let her out of the car. "I can do that myself, ya know? You don't have to open the door for me every time." Clover said matter-of-factly.

"I know you *can*, but I want to, Clover. It's good manners, and I would do this for any of my women friends—not that I have many." I rubbed my neck, hoping I didn't embarrass myself too much.

"And how many women friends do you have, Ryder?" Clover tried her best to look unbothered, but I could see the insecurity cogs starting to turn behind her eyes.

"Two. Mary-Anne and Lois. They are both in their seventies and were my last foster family before I aged out. They taught me manners and tamed my rebellious spirit before it was too late." Clover relaxed, and I took her arm and guided her to the train station. "They are a lesbian couple but never got married, so they could continue to foster kids in Texas. Mary-Anne was technically my only foster parent because they had Lois labeled as her live-in sister. I lived with them from fourteen until I turned eighteen, but still visit them yearly at Christmas."

She smiled, "I'm glad you had them. They sound like lovely people."

I pulled our tickets from the machine, took Clover by the hand, and led her to our terminal. We boarded the orange line in time, sitting in an empty cabin near the back. "Our next stop is Federal Center Southwest if you *must* know," I said mockingly.

Clover turned, sucking her teeth playfully, "I feel your judgment. But at least I can let go of control," she leaned in close, "Can you?" Her tender voice sent tingles across my skin.

I smirked, "Would you like to find out?"

She fought back a smile, biting her lip slightly. "Maybe I would. I want to learn many things about you, Ryder Reed."

"Don't you read the stars? I'm sure you could consult with them, and they would tell you all you want to know about me." Our lips hover over one another once again, and this time, I won't pull back because I need to feel those full lips against mine.

"It's easier to ask the person sitting in front of you rather than the stars." Clover shot back in the same mocking tone I used before.

Her tongue darted across her bottom lip, and I gingerly placed my hand on her neck, idly rubbing the column of her throat with my thumb. "Do you want me to kiss you again, Clover?" She nods, her green eyes begging me, "What if I want you to kiss me?"

Clover hesitated, but it quickly passed, and her lips were on mine.

My mind stilled, and nothing else around us mattered. The only thing on my mind was her. "Clover." I hummed, wrapping my hands in her hair as she straddled me in my seat, placing her hands around my throat. My hands traveled from her hair down to her thighs, squeezing them. She moaned into my mouth as her hands grasped tighter around my throat, driving me insane with desire. I couldn't stop my hands from traveling, and they soon found themselves under her shirt, cupping her breasts. *Fuck!* She's perfect. My hands started to move again, but the announcement for our stop came blaring through the speakers, scaring Clover so bad she jumped back into her seat.

We stared at each other momentarily in shock until we both erupted with laughter.

"That was so out of character of me. I apologize if that was–uh, too much?" Her genuine laughter turned into nervous laughter.

I grabbed her hand, pulled it to my lips, and kissed her knuckles, "Don't apologize, Clover. It wasn't too much." How I wanted to say that I don't think it will ever be enough, and now that I've had a taste, I wanted nothing more than to have her bare before me, body and soul.

But I don't say that because *that* would be *too much*.

Instead, I guided Clover off the train and headed to the place I picked for our date.

8

Clover

"You've brought me to the Botanical Gardens?" I stared up at the Barthholdi Fountain, knowing exactly where I was.

"I heard the rose garden greenhouse is gorgeous at this time of year, but I have another place in mind if this isn't something you'd want to do. " Ryder said, and I could hear the nervousness in his voice.

"I've always wanted to visit the gardens, but I've never had the chance to. I'm so excited!" Ryder pulled my hand up for another kiss, and I swear he was trying to make me swoon.

"Perfect. I was hoping you'd be pleased. Shall we start?" Ryder asked.

"Yes, please. Lead the way."

The butterflies are working *overtime* today.

He took me by the hand, and we walked around each outdoor exhibit. We talked about the flowers and which were our favorites. Our small talk eased my mind about earlier things. I don't know what came over me back on the train. There's something about Ryder that makes me lose all my senses around him. I got into his car after only meeting him the night before, but something was different about Ryder, and I was entirely too *eager* to know more.

We reached the rose garden greenhouse, and I hurried to open the door, beating Ryder to it, "Ha! Now, you have to go through the door first."

Ryder laughed, "You are so stubborn, but it's adorable to watch." I walked through the door behind him, taking his hand in mine, and looked on in awe.

Roses of all colors lined the entire massive greenhouse. It was a sea of red and pink roses with more vibrant yellow, purple, and orange roses towards the back of the room, drawing your attention. "This is the most beautiful thing I've ever seen."

"I would have to agree," Ryder said, smiling down at me, and my face heated. I stared up at him, waiting for the 'just kidding' part like Jason used to do whenever he complimented me, but Ryder just stared back at me. I was snapped back to reality when I heard the booming laughter of children filtering in through the back doors of the rose garden.

I stepped back, my nervous laughter bubbling up, "Sorry."

"Why are you apologizing?" Ryder asked, following behind me as I began walking down the winding pathway of the greenhouse.

"Force of habit, I guess." I wound one of my curls around my finger nervously. "I hope I haven't offended you."

Stupid insecurities. Stop talking, Clover.

Ryder's hand grabbed mine, stopping my fumbling hands. "You've done nothing to offend me, Clover." He laced his fingers through mine, pulling me to him. "Shall we enjoy the rest of the rose garden?" I nodded, now looking at him in awe instead of the roses.

After finishing the tour around the Botanical gardens, Ryder suggested a late lunch. I wholeheartedly agreed, as I was nervous about our date and had not eaten breakfast that morning. He led us a few blocks away to a Korean BBQ restaurant.

"Have you had Koren BBQ before?" Ryder asked, holding the restaurant door open for me. The familiar aroma of sesame oil and chilies had me nearly drooling.

"It's one of my favorites. There was a Koren BBQ place in Waldorf I used to love going to, but it shut down a few years ago." I said as we waited for the hostess to seat us.

Ryder raised his brow, "Really? I thought you would have lived and breathed seafood, seeing as you live on an island."

I laughed, "I love a good Maryland Blue Crab but don't enjoy fish that much." Ryder chuckled, and I saw the hostess coming our way.

"Hello, welcome, for two?" The young woman asked.

Ryder answered, "Yes, please. Thank you."

The hostess led us to a booth, and our server was already there to greet us. As I sat down, Ryder ordered Soju for us, and I began to look over the menu. "This place is nice. I miss this part about living near DC—the food, the atmosphere, and the convenience of having what you want or need within walking distance."

Ryder smirked, "I thought you grew up in Solomons Island?"

I gave him a half smile, "I did. My parents lived there for most of my life, but towards the end of their addiction, we moved closer to DC. We lived in a one-bedroom apartment in District Heights for two years. My Aunt and Uncle brought me back to Solomons after they died. I don't remember much of my time in District Heights, but the parts I do remember always involved food." I bit my lip, fearing I said too much or was too blunt.

Iris is always getting on me about my bluntness.

"Do you miss them?" Ryder asked sincerely, and it stunned me.

Most guys would have run the other way by now, listening to me ramble about my dead parents, but Ryder is *different*. "I miss who they were and who they could have been. But their love for drugs was stronger, and they weren't the parents I once knew. I grieved them long before they died."

Our server came back, lighting the grill in front of us, and poured a glass of Soju for each of us. We ordered what we wanted from the menu, and Ryder slid closer to me in the booth. I can feel my heartbeat in my neck already, and he hasn't even touched me. Having him close to me already makes me lose all my senses, and now that alcohol is involved, who knows what I'll say or do?

He's just a man, Clover. Calm down.

A really, *really* sexy man, but he is still a man at his core. Stand *up*, girl!

I laughed to myself, and Ryder smirked, "What's so funny?" He asked.

"Oh, nothing." I smiled, twirling my curl absent-mindedly around my finger.

Ryder picked up the curl I was playing with and brought it to his lips. "Do I make you nervous, Clover?"

"Yes," I admitted. "In a good way." My chest heaved, and I felt almost breathless.

He dropped my curl, picked up my hand in its place, and kissed my knuckles softly, "In a good way, how?" Ryder asked.

I swallowed, "I've never met anyone like you. You're adventurous and free-spirited. You know what you want, and you go for it. I've only known you two days, but you've shown me a lot of who you are, and it scares me if I'm honest." Ryder turned my hand over, kissing the inside of my wrist.

If I could melt, I would have on the spot.

"Why does it scare you?" He asked, giving me a look of concern rather than a distaste for my honesty.

"Because good things don't usually happen to me, Ryder. The moment I felt a crumb of happiness in the past, something was always waiting in the shadows to snatch it away." I admitted.

I blame the Soju for my honesty.

Ryder lowered my hand but still held it firm in his. "I will be whatever you want me to be, Clover. If you want this to be a fling, I'll leave quietly at the end of my eight-week stay, and you'll never hear from me again." I felt a lump in my throat at the mention of him leaving. "Or we can go slow and see where this takes us, and at the end of my eight weeks, we can talk more seriously. I want you, Clover. Friend, lover, or husband, I'll take you any way you have me."

I snorted, "Husband? Aren't you getting a little ahead of yourself?" I pulled my hand away, gulping the Soju, as Ryder relaxed in the booth.

"Maybe I am, but a man can dream?" Ryder said, making my face heat.

The server arrived, once again saving me from embarrassment, and laid out an assortment of meats, veggies, and dipping sauces.

Ryder grabbed his chopsticks and began grilling some of the meat. The aroma was just as I remembered, and my stomach remembered.

I'm thankful for the music the restaurant is playing because I'm pretty sure my stomach was singing.

Ryder pulled the first piece of meat off, dipped it in one of the sauces, and held it out for me to take. The moment it touched my tongue, I couldn't stop the moan that escaped my mouth. It was heavenly. The meat was tender and full of flavor.

I hadn't realized Ryder was staring at me, and I felt my face heat again. "Here, try this next." He grabbed some kimchi, and I happily obliged.

I groaned, "That is the best kimchi I have ever had. Your turn to try." I grabbed my chopsticks, scooped some up, and fed it to Ryder.

He let out a satisfied groan of his own. "That is excellent kimchi."

We continued like this, feeding each other one after the other and chatting until our meal was gone. I let out a satisfied hum, and Ryder chuckled, "Did you enjoy your meal, Clover?"

I smiled. "Very much so. Thank you for bringing me here, Ryder. And the Garden, that was special."

"The pleasure is all mine," Ryder said, winking.

With impeccable timing, the server came over with our check, and Ryder handed them his credit card without even looking at the bill first. "What do you want to do next? I saw a gelato shop close by that had some good reviews."

"You're just spoiling me now." I laughed, but Ryder

just smiled. Something in me clicked, and I decided to stop overthinking things and just do. "I would love to get some gelato with you. That sounds perfect."

Ryder's smile widened, "Perfect."

9

Ryder

We finished our desserts and ordered coffee as Clover and I sat at the gelato shop, swapping stories of our youth and getting to know each other more.

"I was always on the water growing up—whether at the beach or on a boat, the bay calls my name. This one time at the beginning of summer, my friends and I went over to Drum Point Beach for the day, and after we were done, we swam across the bay over to Solomons. My aunt caught us while we were swimming up to her dock and nearly rang all of our necks." Clover laughed, "Were you adventurous in Texas like you are now?"

I smirked, "I was definitely *not* as adventurous as you, Clover. I was a quiet kid in school, meaning other kids tried to bully me, and moving became a regular thing for me. Fighting the bullies was highly frowned upon. It wasn't until I lived with Mary-Anne and Lois that I made real friends. They lived on a working farm, so I was up at five in the morning feeding livestock with my foster brother and sister, Micheal and Tina. I eventually opened up to them and stopped being so angsty." Clover smiled, her big, doe green eyes giving me a look of sincerity. "Micheal and Tina helped heal the angry parts of me. Being shifted from home to home messes with your mental state, and I had no idea I was depressed. They were the first to tell me I wasn't alone in my feelings and wouldn't be the last."

"Do you miss them?" Clover asked.

"I do. I haven't seen Micheal or Tina since they left the farm. They aged out of the foster system. Micheal left first, and then Tina soon behind him. I tried to find them once I left the farm, hoping to reconnect in our adulthood, but with no luck." Clover gave me a half-smile but looked down at her bag and pulled out her buzzing phone.

"I'm sorry, it's Iris. I'll be right back." Clover got up from the table and walked out the front door of the gelato shop. She was still in eyeshot, and I couldn't help but watch her. Clover answered her phone with a smile, but the more she talked to Iris, the more I noticed her smile fading and turning into a look of worry. The phone call was quick, and she returned with the worried look now gone. "Sorry about that." She said as she sat down, forcing a smile.

"Is everything okay?" I couldn't stop myself from asking.

The look on her face said that something had happened, and I wanted to help if I could.

Clover sighed, "Iris flooded the bathroom upstairs on accident. Unfortunately, my bedroom is next to the bathroom, so my room was the most affected." Her eyes darted around the room, avoiding eye contact.

I don't know why, but I felt like Clover wasn't telling me the whole truth. "I could help you clean up when we return," I suggested.

"No!" She shouted, "Sorry–no, thank you. Iris and Aiden have already started to clean up, and they called a carpet-cleaning company to clean the carpet upstairs in the morning. Thank you for the offer, though." Clover said while folding her arms across her chest and rubbing her arms.

She was self-soothing. Something must have happened, and Clover wasn't ready to tell me. "How about I get a hotel for us here in the city for the night? I will book a separate room if that suits you better. You look like you're having fun, and I don't want the date to end if I'm being honest." It was the truth. I didn't want this date to end, but Clover looks like she also doesn't want to go home.

"You keep surprising me, Ryder." Clover looked me up and down, biting her bottom lip slightly, and, Oh, how I wished it was me biting it instead. "I will call Iris back and tell her I won't be home tonight. Look up a bar while I'm gone. I think I need a stronger drink."

I smiled, "As you wish." Clover was out the front, calling Iris again.

I paid our bill and looked up a hotel and bar in the area. I found one a few blocks away and booked two rooms just in case. The bar attached to the hotel was well-reviewed and seemed a staple in the area. I left the gelato shop to find Clover still on the phone.

"Is it bad? Did he destroy anything else?" The use of the word he catches my attention, but Clover notices me and quickly tells Iris goodbye, "Oh, I gotta go. Love you. Bye." Clover walked over to me and laced her fingers through mine. "So, where are we going?" she asked.

"There's a hotel down the street with a bar. Two birds, one stone," I said, and Clover laughed.

God, how I loved hearing that.

"But I have somewhere I want to take you first before we head there," I said, taking her hand in mine.

"Oh, you do? Well, lead the way, Mr. Mysterious." Clover said, and I laughed at my new nickname.

The Uber Black I ordered pulled up next to us, and I opened the door for her, "Your chariot awaits."

10

Clover

Ryder helped me onto the black escalade that pulled up. Ryder sat next to me, lifted his arm over me, and draped it over the backseat as I put my seatbelt on. His smokey ember scent hit me again, and I unapologetically basked in it. I shut my eyes, taking him in, and when I opened them, Ryder looked at me with amusement.

"What?" I asked, but it came out breathy. He was already close to me, but I could feel him moving closer. Our noses were almost touching before he stopped.

"Can I kiss you again?" Ryder asked, only saying it loud enough for me to hear. I raised my hand, cupping his face, and pulled him in for a kiss without a second thought. His kisses are soft and gentle, and they make my heart feel like it is doing flips in my chest. It was as if he had stolen all the air from my lungs and replaced it with his own.

Ryder's fingers teased up my thigh, resting on my hip. I bit Ryder's bottom lip, giving it a little tug, and he moaned against my mouth. "You are playing with fire, Clover," Ryder whispered as he gently squeezed my hip, sending a wave of pleasure to my core.

"Maybe I want to get burned, Ryder," I said breathlessly. "Maybe I like to play with fire."

Ryder let go of my hip and caressed my face, "You're too beautiful to burn. You deserve *worship*, Clover."

The Uber came to a stop, and Ryder stepped out first, leaving me in a daze in the back seat. He handed our driver a tip as I tried to gather what was left of my frazzled brain. I stepped out of the escalade to see that Ryder had brought us to CityCenterDC. It's a shopping center with designer stores like Louis Vuitton and Christian Louboutin. "This is a very fancy shopping center, Ryder. Did you mean to bring us here?"

Surely, he meant to bring us to Galley Place?

The Uber takes off, and he joins me at my side. "We have a reservation tonight at the bar, and neither of us can show up in what we have on, so I figured we needed new clothes," Ryder said nonchalantly.

"But these are really expensive stores, and I live on a bartender's budget." I was sweating, even considering the price tags on a pair of socks, let alone a *dress*, in one of these stores.

He's crazy if he thought I was going to buy clothes here.

"I didn't say anything about you paying, either. It's my treat." Ryder said, cocking his eyebrow.

I shook my head, "No, Ryder. You've already paid for everything. This is too much. We can go to Gallery Place after you get your clothes, and I can find something there. Plus, these stores don't carry my size. Save us both from embarrassment." I ramble when I'm nervous, which lets some insecurities slip.

"Let's walk around and see if we find a store you want to try. If we don't find anything here, we will go to Gallery Place." He lifted my hand to his lips, "I promise."

"Fine. But don't get your hopes up." I said as I pulled Ryder toward where the shopping center started.

We walked around the center for about twenty minutes before I could see the last row of shops before the Center ended. I passed all the high-end designer stores, knowing they would not carry dresses for my size sixteen womanly body. I have a shapely body, and I'm damn proud of it, and I wouldn't let any of these stores define my worth—but the longer we walk, the more *shame*

I feel. It didn't help the store employees gave me the 'Don't even think about it, fatty' face through the store windows. I almost gave up hope, but at the end of the row of shops, I saw a familiar logo for a plus-size luxury brand I had seen in a magazine a few months back. "Can we go in here?" I asked Ryder, pointing to the storefront.

"Of course," Ryder said and moved to open the door for me.

Ryder's chivalry was genuinely unmatched, and I couldn't help but notice how my heart skipped a beat when he did things for me just because he could and wanted to.

Unlike all other stores, I walked through the door and was greeted by a beautiful female employee with a noticeable smile. "Hi, welcome to Sante Grace. I'm Greta. Could I help you find anything today?" Greta asked.

I opened my mouth to say no and that we would just look around, but Ryder spoke up behind me, "She does. We have a reservation for dinner at Fiola tonight and would love your help."

"Oh, how lovely. Come with me—what is your name, beautiful?" Greta asked, taking me by the arm and leading me through clothes racks.

"I'm Clover," I said, half-smiling her.

"What kind of style are you looking for tonight? Have you ever shopped with us before?" Greta asked as she continued to guide me through the store to the back, where a waiting area was. Ryder sat down, making himself comfortable on the creme-colored couches.

"I haven't shopped here before, but everything looks so beautiful. And as far as style, I am at your mercy, Greta." I said nervously.

"Oh, I'm so happy you said that because we have this green slip dress that I know would look amazing on you. Head back there," she pointed to a doorway at the back of the room concealed with a curtain. "That's the fitting room. I will come back shortly with a couple of options for you."

"Okay, thank you," I said while heading to the fitting room. I smiled at Ryder, who gave me an encouraging wave.

I entered the fitting room, closing the heavy luxury curtain that separated the room behind me.

The room was large, with a mirrored wall at the back and a podium in the middle to get a full three sixty of the outfits you'd try on. Greta knocked on the wall, peeking her head in, holding what looked like four or five dresses. "Are you ready for me?" She asked.

"Yes, thank you," I said, gesturing to her. Greta opened the curtain and began hanging the dresses she brought in for me to try on the hooks anchored to the side wall.

One dress she brought immediately caught my eye. It was an emerald green slip dress with spaghetti straps and a scoop neckline. I gravitated towards it, picking up the fabric in my hands to feel its silky texture, and I was not disappointed. It felt *rich*. The dress felt like luxurious butter in my hands, and I *really* wanted to try it on.

"That is the dress I had in mind for you. Do you like it?" Greta asked, closing the curtain again and coming over to me.

"I do. I like it very much." I answered, my fingers still playing with the fabric.

"Good. That is the first one we will try." Greta picked up the dress and guided me to the podium.

"I'm sorry, but how do you know that it will fit me? I didn't tell you my size," I asked in earnest.

Greta turned to me, "It's my job, dear. Size sixteen, right?" My mouth popped open to reply, but I shut it instead and just nodded.

She was good.

Greta helped me out of my clothes and into the dress, which fit like a glove. I turned to face the mirror and gasped. It was like this dress was made for me. The neckline complimented the shape of my chest, and how the fabric cascaded down and hugged every curve of my body made it look ethereal. "You look amazing, Clover." I smiled at Greta's kind words but couldn't take my eyes off myself. "Shall we go show Mr. Ryder?" Greta asked.

I looked myself up and down once more, "Yes. I think Mr.

Ryder will be *very* pleased." Devious thoughts about what Ryder would do once we were alone ran through my head, but I shook them away as Greta led me back out of the fitting room.

"Close your eyes!" I shouted loud enough for Ryder to hear.

"Got it. My eyes are closed." Ryder shouted back.

Greta guided me to the fitting podium in front of the couch where Ryder was sitting. "No peeking," Greta said as she fixed my hair and smoothed the dress. "Okay, Mr. Ryder, you can open them now."

Ryder opened his eyes, and his mouth immediately fell open. "Holy fuck. I mean—wow. You look *incredible*, Clover."

"Do you like it? It feels amazing. Do you think it's too much for dinner?" I felt nervous under his gaze, but his eyes stayed locked on mine.

"I think you should own one in every color. The dress looks like it was made for you," Ryder answered, looking me up and down. A deep warmth spread around my core.

God, he knew how to make my knees weak.

"She will need shoes to match and a handbag if you have any," Ryder said to Greta.

"I have the perfect match already picked out," Greta answered.

"Good," Ryder said, handing her his credit card. "And any accessories—a necklace and some earrings should do."

"Of course, Mr. Ryder. I will be right back." Greta turned, giving me a wink, and I couldn't help but laugh.

"Something funny?" Ryder asked. I looked at him, and he was already close to me. His hands grabbed my hips, pulling me to him.

I draped my arms around his shoulders, his lips hovering so close to mine I could smell his minty, sweet breath. "I was just thinking how good this dress would look on the floor of our hotel room later."

Ryder hummed, "Oh, is that so?" His hands traveled around to my ass, giving it a firm squeeze, "That's a sight I'd kill to see."

I laughed again, running my finger lazily up his bare arm,

"Maybe you will."

◆ ◆ ◆

After paying for my new clothes, Ryder and I walked to Brioni next door to purchase his suit. This designer store screamed luxury and smelled like it. It had a musky, masculine scent that a wealthy businessperson would wear. It reminded me of this group of businessmen who vacationed in Solomon's last summer. They were rowdy and flaunted their wealth by buying out the bar almost every night at Sunset.

An older gentleman greeted us, and Ryder immediately introduced himself as they began chatting about suits. I took to the floor, looking over all the different suit options. They had several tables at the front with sale signs on them. I flipped over the tag on one of the dress shirts they had folded on the table, which read *Twelve Hundred Dollars*. My eyes nearly bulged out of my head.

Ryder must have a *substantial* expendable income.

I flipped the tag back over and kept my hands to myself as I looked through the rest of the store.

Ryder returned moments later and asked, "What do you think?" I turned to find him in an all-black suit with a silky emerald green tie. He looked like he had just stepped off the runway for Giorgio Armani.

I had to pick my jaw up from the floor before I could reply. "I love it. You look amazing. The tie is a nice touch." I caught my bottom lip between my teeth, looking him up and down.

I wasn't trying to hide it, either.

"I'll take it, Ewan. Thank you." Ryder said to the older gentlemen.

"Of course, Mr. Reed. I will charge it to your account." Ewan handed Ryder a bag and an iPad, which he scribbled on, handing the iPad back to Ewan.

Ryder checked the back before making his way over to me.

"Are you ready to go?" Ryder asked as he fixed the strap on my dress, running his fingers idly down my exposed back.

"Yes, Mr. Reed," I said seductively.

"Oh, you are wicked, Clover," Ryder said as I wrapped my arm around his, giggling at my accomplished tease. "The Uber will be here shortly. Come on, this way." He smirked and led me out of the store.

11

Ryder

Due to traffic, we arrived at the hotel later than expected and almost missed our dinner reservation. Thankfully, the restaurant was in the hotel, so we didn't have far to go once we got there. The dinner at Fiola was rather good, but I much preferred the view. I couldn't stop staring at Clover. She looked so ethereal. She sipped on her second glass of champagne; her lips caressed the glass, and I watched her swallow the bubbly liquid. I followed the column of her neck, straight down the length of her body, and—*Jesus fucking Christ*.

I motioned to the waiter for the check and adjusted *myself*. I usually have better control, but I remembered the kiss we shared earlier in the Uber, and now I'm rock hard. The waiter arrived with the check just as Clover finished her drink. I handed him my card, and he took off with it promptly.

Clover leaned forward, her elbows perched on the table, and I swallowed hard, trying to keep my composure. "Where to now?" She asked.

I cleared my throat, "Eager to leave, Clover?"

She laughed, "No, I'm eager to dance with you, Ryder." Clover teasingly rubbed her foot up the side of my calf.

My dick was screaming at me to take her upstairs, but my brain knew that was not what she wanted. She wanted to dance.

The waiter returned, and I stood from the table, holding my hand out to her, "Let's dance then." She gleefully took my hand,

and I led her out of the restaurant and to the elevators. We didn't wait long before the ding of the elevator arrived, and we stepped in. I pressed the button 'B' for the basement.

"The nightclub is in the basement?" Clover asked.

"It is. It's called 'The Abyss', one of the highest-rated clubs in DC."

Clover giggled, "The Abyss sounds quite ominous. Its name reminds me of a club you'd find in a vampire book." The elevator's ding sounded, and the doors opened to a lounge.

Several people lined the bar, while others sat around tables quietly, having conversations. At the back of the room, two security guards stood at the entrance to the club.

"This is the nightclub?" Clover asked. Her worried tone made me chuckle.

"No. The club is through those doors at the back. This is for hotel guests only. It's a private lounge." I took her hand in mine and led her over to the bar. "Do you want a drink?"

"Yes, please. I'll take a Mojito," she said, and I let go of her hand, leaving her momentarily to place our drink order with the bartender.

The man behind the bar started making our drinks, and I turned to find an older gentleman trying to make a move on Clover. She declined whatever he asked her for, and he walked away with a bruised ego.

"Here are your drinks. Which room should I charge them to, sir?" The bartender asked.

"Room 2504," I said, taking our drinks off the bar, "Thank you." I gave him a nod and turned to find Clover surrounded by men. "Excuse me, gentlemen. Clover," I handed her her drink and wrapped my free arm around her waist, guiding her past them.

Clover took a few gulps of her Mojitio, "Thank you. That was so scary. They came out of nowhere." She laughed nervously.

I pulled her into me, "I wouldn't let anything happen to you." She smiled and took another sip of her drink. The security guards at the doors spoke to someone over an earpiece before he opened the doors for us. The loud booming of club music filled the lounge. "Have a good evening," the security guard said as he waved us through.

Steps led down to a door, but from the top of the steps, you could see the crowd of people below.

Lights flashed, and the bodies of those below grinded with one another in a heated frenzy to the beat. I guided Clover down the steps and exited the club's doors. The music was so loud I could barely hear Clover of the music, "Come dance with me!" She shouted into my ear.

I tossed back the rest of my old-fashioned and set it on the nearest table. "Lead the way," I said.

Clover took me by the hand, pushing our way through the crowd. I wiggled my hand free from hers and took her by the hips, holding her to me as she wrapped her arms around my neck. I adjusted my hands to the small of her back as she swayed to the beat against me. Clover pulled back, taking a sip from her drink. I spun her around so that her ass was grinding against me, and I spoke against her ear, "I can feel every man's eyes on you. I can see in their eyes how badly they wished they were me. I love watching them watch you, knowing they could never satisfy you how I can." Clover's breath hitched, and she tried to face me, but I held her firm. I kissed her neck softly, "Let them watch. It's the only thing they can do. Enjoy yourself, Clover. Dance."

Clover set her now empty cup on a tray of cups a club employee was carrying. She turned to face me, wrapping her arms around my neck again. Her hips swayed to the beat of the music, and I felt entranced. I couldn't take my eyes off her. Clover truly embodies a Greek goddess deserving of being sculpted.

Painted.

Worshipped.

Clover looked up at me, flashing a sinful smile, and it all but took my breath away. "Follow me. I see an empty booth." She said into my ear. I did as she said and followed her to a booth. It wasn't long before a waitress came around and asked if we needed anything.

"Yes! Four shots of vodka, please." Clover answered. The

waitress nodded and took off into the crowd.

"Four shots?" I asked, surprised. Clover slid beside me, and I couldn't stop myself from touching her. My hand slid from her knee, up her thigh, and landed on her hip.

Clover tipped my face to hers. "I like ending my night with a *bang*." She caught her bottom lip in her teeth, and it felt like my heart stopped. My body buzzed all over as she leaned closer to me. The waitress returned with our order, breaking our entanglement, and I told her to charge it to our room. The waitress nodded and disappeared back into the crowd. I turned my attention back to Clover, and she had two shots in her hands and a wicked grin, "For you," she said as she handed me the shot, "Cheers! To new beginnings."

Clover raised her glass, and we clinked them together, "To new beginnings." I watched Clover bring hers to her lips first and followed suit.

She hissed as she picked up the second round of shots, handing me mine, "This one is for us. We survived all the odds and somewhat came out on top. We deserve to cheers to that."

My words got caught up in my throat, and for the first time, I was speechless. I held my glass up, "To us." Clover smiled, and I watched as she took her shot. But I still sat as I tried to keep my heart from beating out of my chest.

Clover is selfless and pure of heart, and I am quickly falling for her.

I regained control of my heart, and I took the shot, hissing at the burning sensation it left behind.

A song caught Clover's attention, and she took me by the hand as she shuffled out of the booth, "Come on! It's Rihanna! We have to dance!" I laughed as I quickly followed behind her.

She pulled me to her and wrapped her arms around my neck like before, but this time, it was different. Her energy was erratic, and her movements were more precise.

If I didn't know any better, I would think she was trying to turn me on.

I chuckled as I came to the realization and pulled her tight to me, our bodies grinding on top of each other, and I let her feel just how turned on I was.

Clover gasped and leaned into me, "Take me upstairs, Ryder, please."

I pulled away to see her face, "Are you sure?"

Clover nodded, "Please." She wrapped her arms around my neck and kissed me. I took her face in my hands and deepened the kiss. We both pulled away, dazed and panting. She smiled up at me, and I pulled her hands from around my neck, kissing her knuckles, and started pulling her toward the stairs.

"Let's get you upstairs then, shall we?" Clover's smile is enough of an answer for me, and we head upstairs.

12

Clover

The lounge is nearly empty as we pass through to the elevators. Another couple is waiting for the elevators, dampening my excitement about being alone in the elevator with Ryder. His hand is on the small of my back, and his fingers trace idly as we wait.

Everything about Ryder makes my body feel electric. I am drawn to him in ways I have never been drawn to anyone. I never expected to fall so hard for him, but here I am. It's ridiculous to say something like that about someone you just met, especially with how my last relationship went, but I feel safe with Ryder.

The ding of the elevator sounded, and the doors slid open. The couple before us first walked in and pressed the level seven floor. Ryder pressed the number twenty-five, and my heart skipped a little. He stood at the back of the elevator, holding his hand out for me to take. He pulled me into him, wrapping his arm around my waist and resting his lips against my bare neck. I held back my gasp and bit my lip. I turned to him and shook my head. Ryder only smiled down at me, and I bit my lip harder, holding back my smile.

The elevator began to rise, and I felt Ryder's hand drift to my thigh. He played with the edge of my dress, and I relaxed into him. His lips grazed my neck again, and I was putty in his hands.

He could strip me naked right here with this couple watching, and I wouldn't care.

The elevator dinged, and I quickly straightened myself,

pulling away from Ryder. The couple walked off, and the doors closed. I could feel Ryder behind me, and I watched him reach for the number board on the elevator. He pressed twenty-five again but held it down until the elevator started moving again. I turned to face him, and he was already moving, grabbing my face in his hands and spinning me around with my back against the wall. His hands left my face and found their way to my hips as I pulled myself up and wrapped my legs around Ryder's waist.

"Wait," Ryder said, lowering me. "I need to say something." I stared up at Ryder, my breath uneven and ragged and my heart pounding in my ears. "I don't want this to be a one-time thing. I want you, Clover. You deserve to be loved, and I want to be the person who shows you exactly how you should be treated. If you don't want that, say the word, and this stops."

I closed the distance between us, and it was my turn to bring his face to mine, "I want this. I want you, too, Ryder."

It's the truth. I can't deny this attraction I feel towards him.

Ryder leaned into me, our lips hovering centimeters apart. "Then kiss me."

I was captivated by him. Our energy is magnetic, and I'm tired of fighting the pull I feel toward Ryder. I know it's sudden, and all of this could be fake, but it's what I want.

Our lips met in the heat of passion, and I don't know which of us moved first, but it didn't matter because we were clawing at each other now. The ding of the elevator reaching our floor sounded, dragging our attention to the now-open doors. Ryder smiled, taking me by the hand and leading us down the hall.

It was more like dragging me down the hall because I was so giddy from all the alcohol.

Ryder unlocked the door to our room, and I stumbled past him, entering the room first. I kicked off my shoes at the door, threw my purse down with them, and walked into the room. My jaw nearly hit the floor when I saw the view we had. Our room has a floor-to-ceiling window, with a king-size bed in the middle. I couldn't resist looking out the window and gasped at how high we were. Thinking back to the elevator, I think there were only twenty-seven floors in this hotel.

Looking down at the street, my knees felt wobbly, but Ryder slid his arms around my middle, keeping me steady. He kissed my exposed neck, and I let out a soft moan.

Ryder held me with one arm as his other hand slowly crept up my body, teasing my nipple as he passed it. His hand found the strap of my dress, and he slid it off my shoulder. I slipped my arm out of the strap, and my dress shifted, exposing my breast. Ryder shifted his stance and dropped my other arm out of the dress, and I watched as it floated to the floor in a luxurious pile of silk. I see myself in the window's reflection and notice Ryder doing the same.

"Perfection," Ryder said softly in my ear. His hands explored my body as I watched in the reflection. Ryder dragged his fingers lightly all over my body, toying at the edges of my black thong. His right hand teased its way from my hip to just below my belly button. I sucked in a breath as Ryder's hand pushed passed my thong, and he began to rub my clit.

"Oh!" I gasped, and Ryder grinned.

"You're so wet, Clover, and I've barely touched you." Ryder slipped a finger in my pussy, and I gasped again. His free hand found my throat, and he held me as he slid his finger in and out painfully slow. "Do you want to come, Clover?"

"Yes, please, Ryder, make me come. I want you to make me come." I made eye contact with him in the window, and he slipped two fingers inside me this time. "Ryder!" I gasped, and my head fell back in ecstasy. I held on to his arm at my throat as he fingered my pussy. "Yes, Ryder, right there! Don't stop!" He picked up his pace, sliding his fingers in and out rapidly.

"Come for me, Clover. I want this pretty pussy to soak my hand." Ryder said into my ear, his voice low and demanding. His rapid movements slowed as he buried his fingers deep inside me, pulsing them as the palm of his hand rubbed my clit.

I lifted onto my tip toes as Ryder drew my orgasm out, "I'm coming! Fuck!" Ryder's grip tightened around my neck, and I came hard. He let go of my neck as I came down from the high

I was on, and I spun around after I gained my footing and began unbuttoning his shirt.

Ryder smirked, "Need more, don't you, Clover?"

"Yes," I said, but it came out breathy as I tried to kiss him, but he pulled away from me.

Ryder scooped me up under my legs and carried me to the bed. He slowly removed his shirt, pieces of his dark hair framed his face, and my mouth dried.

This man looks sculpted by the gods, with his eight-pack abs and abdominal V-lines that I wanted to run my tongue over.

Ryder looked me up and down as he undid his belt. The swoosh of the leather belt moving through the loops of his pants and the metal buckle thudding to the floor made my pussy drip wet with anticipation. He pushed his suit pants to the floor, and I perched on my elbows, watching him. Ryder sank to his knees, pushing my legs open, and kissed his way down my thigh. My head rolled back, and I let out a soft moan. I could feel his breath on my pussy, and when I looked down, his eyes met mine, and I watched as his tongue darted out between his lips and licked my clit. I hissed as he stopped with just one lick. I squirmed, trying to get closer to him to make him do it again.

"So very needy," Ryder said in a low, seductive tone that made my hair stand on end. "Such a pretty pussy. Forgive me for admiring such beauty." His words were direct, and my cheeks flushed.

Our eyes met again, but this time, I watched as he began to lap up my pussy.

I watched as Ryder sucked and fingered my pussy to the edge of bliss.

I watched as he coaxed orgasm after orgasm out of me.

"I need you, Ryder," I admitted, breathless. Ryder smiled, wiping the corners of his mouth, and stood. I stared up at him as he pushed his boxers to the floor, his cock now on full display. I licked my lips, capturing my bottom lip between my teeth.

He closed the distance between us, hovering over me but still standing at the edge of the bed, "Are you sure you want this?

We can stop now if you've changed your mind." Ryder said.

I gathered his face in my hands, looking deep into his eyes. "I want you, Ryder. I want this. I want us."

Ryder pushed his way onto the bed and kissed me. The kiss was hard and starved as all the air in the room vanished, and we only had each other's air to breathe. Ryder pulled back, grabbing his cock and teasing my entrance, rubbing the tip of his cock against my sensitive clit. "Ryder," I breathed, "Please," Ryder answered my plea with one swift thrust as he entered my pussy. We both gasped, staring into each other eyes. He pushed his cock in further, and I moaned loudly, feeling his cock fill me up.

"Fuck, Clover. Your pussy is so warm and tight." Ryder pulled back slowly, watching himself fuck me and fill me. "Such a good girl. You are being so patient for me." Another slow pullback, making my eyes roll back. Ryder grabbed both my legs behind the knees, pushing them upwards making me fall onto my back. He pinned my legs to the bed, picking up his pace.

"Fuck, Ryder! Yes!" I moaned. I felt the pressure of my orgasm rising in my belly as Ryder fucked me. He rocked back and forth, effortlessly pumping his cock into my pussy as I held onto the bed, screaming his name over and over again. Ryder's moans echoed my own, and soon we came together.

Ryder kissed me softly, whispering sweet words and embracing me. "Shower with me?" he asked, his smile saying he wasn't done with me yet.

I smiled back, "Lead the way."

13

Clover

I wake to the smell of freshly brewed coffee, my eyes slowly opening to the brightly lit hotel room. I stretched out in bed, my body deliciously sore from a night of pure bliss. I stared up at the ceiling, remembering last night with Ryder.

We had sex in the shower after the first time and again after we got out.

He was *insatiable*. It's like some sex demon possessed him, and my orgasms were the cure.

The bathroom door slid open, Ryder poked his head out, and I sat up in the bed. "I didn't think you'd be awake yet. I had coffee delivered to the room and a full breakfast for us." His towel hung around his waist, and I soaked up his godly image.

I smiled, "You think of everything."

Ryder walked over to me, smiling, and sat on the edge of the bed next to me. My heart fluttered as he looked into my eyes. "Anything for you, Clover."

I swallowed the emotion in the back of my throat his words caused and said, "Thank you. Yesterday was amazing, to say the least."

Ryder chuckled, and I couldn't hide my smile. "Yes, it was, wasn't it?" He leaned in close, placing a small kiss on my lips, and let out a gruff moan. "Breakfast first. I am starved." I laughed as Ryder got up from the bed, making his way over to the kitchenette in our room. "How do you take your coffee?"

"Three sugars and two half-and-half, please, and thank you." Ryder nodded, and I got up from the bed, wrapping the loose sheet around me as I searched for my phone.

My backpack, which we checked at the front desk last night when we checked into the hotel, was sitting on the sofa across the room. I crossed the room, picked up the bag, and rummaged through it until I found my phone. I tapped the side button to wake it, and two messages from Iris popped up on the screen.

The first message confirmed that Jason had broken in and trashed the place and that she had cleaned up our house. The second message was the security footage from our neighbors across the street, catching Jason entering my house, exiting ten minutes later, and getting into a Jeep that took off down the street. I shook my head, feeling defeated, and put my phone back in my backpack.

I wanted to stay in this blissful bubble a bit longer before I had to pop it.

Ryder sat at the table, and I joined him, trying to shake off Iris's messages. Ryder placed a plate of a full traditional American breakfast in front of me, "Nothing better than eggs and bacon in the morning."

I laughed, "I'm inclined to agree. I love bacon." I picked a piece up off my plate and bit an end off, groaning at its lustful, salty maple flavor, "Yummy."

"A woman after my heart," Ryder said, picking up a piece from his plate and biting. "Would you like to do anything today before we head back?"

And here comes the bubble pop.

"As much as I want to stay up here, I have to get back home. I promised I'd help Iris out today at the beach." It wasn't an entire lie, but it was a lie, and it made me feel icky. I can't tell him about Jason. I can handle him on my own. Ryder doesn't need to get involved with my life drama, especially if we don't work out.

"No problem. We will head out after breakfast." He smiled, taking another bite of his food, and that icky feeling pulled at me, but I shoved a forkful full of eggs in my mouth in the hope of shoving down that icky feeling.

◆ ◆ ◆

It was almost noon before we got back to Solomons. Ryder pulled into his driveway, shutting the car off as we sat silently. I fidgeted with my cuticles, unsure of what to say.

"I meant what I said, Clover," I looked up from my hands, his expression soft, "I want to give us a chance, do you? If your mind has changed, I will humbly accept your answer."

My mind told me to wait, but my heart was saying yes.

I was falling faster than I wanted, which scared and excited me. I had never felt this close to Jason, and Jason had never made me feel the way Ryder does. I wanted something different, and Ryder was different. I wanted to listen to my heart this time. "I do. I want to give us a chance, Ryder."

He leaned forward, pressing a kiss to my lips, "I will hear you say 'I do' again one day." My cheeks heated, and a smile spread across my face. "Iris is waiting in the driveway. You better go. I'll text you." Ryder said, caressing my cheek.

I looked in the rearview mirror and saw Iris at the end of our driveway with her arms crossed. I sighed, "Yeah, I should. She's going to ask me a million questions."

Ryder chuckled, "Don't get me demoted with all the dirty details."

I laughed, "Oh, she will hear an earful today."

Ryder grabbed my hand, pulling up to his lips, "Come over tonight?"

I smiled, my heart swelling in my chest. "Maybe. I'll text you." He nodded and let go of my hand.

I opened the car door and heard Iris, "Hurry up, Clover! We need to be at the beach in thirty minutes!"

"I'm coming!" I shouted back.

Ryder smiled, "Funny, I heard the same thing last night. Over. And over. And over." He handed me my bag, and I stifled my laugh. "Have a good day," he said, winking.

"Goodbye, Ryder." I caught my bottom lip between my teeth and shut the car door.

I walked over to Iris, and she was already giddy, "How was your night last night?" she asked.

"It was...the best night I've ever had," I admitted.

Iris giggled, took my hand, and waved to Ryder, who was getting out of his car. I urged Iris into the house, giving one last look over my shoulder at him as I shut the door.

"Okay, spill. You have freshly fucked hair." Iris said. I laughed, and when I gave no response, Iris's face turned wicked. "Shut up! What does that mean? Are you guys together?"

"Well. I wouldn't say that. Ryder's here temporarily on business, but we *are* seeing each other while he's here. And if it goes well, potentially be long distance? I don't know. We didn't iron out the details."

Iris laughed, "Yeah, too busy ironing you out, it seems."

"That he did. Multiple times." I bit back, and the look on Iris's face was worth it.

"Oh, I like this, Clover. She's fierce." Iris sighed, "Did you see the video I sent?"

"I did. Jason and his buddies are still trying to scare me."

And it worked. But I wasn't going to admit that.

"What are we going to do about it?" Iris asked.

"There's not much I can do, Iz. You know who he is and who his family is. I'll email his father the security footage and make him have a conversation with him." I said, feeling defeated.

I don't think it will do much, but at least he knows he can get caught if he does anything like that again.

"Clo, he's drinking again. He has put his hands on you. What's stopping him from doing it again? His daddy? He's been back in town for less than a week, and he's already broken the promise he gave his father. I'm scared for you, Clo. I think you should take this to the police."

I huffed, "And what? Have them laugh in my face like last time? Iris, come on, you know I can't." I tried to go to the police to get a restraining order put on Jason after he punched me, and the officer at the desk was Jason's old college buddy. He refused to do anything and had me escorted out of the building. It was the first time I realized how deep Jason's hold was on everyone in this town. He was a good ol' boy, and I was the town addict's daughter. "I wish I could do something, Iz. You know I would if I could."

Iris laced her fingers in mine and pulled me to the couch in the living room. She put her arms around me and cuddled me close, "I'm sorry. I know you would. I'm just scared."

"I'm sorry you had to go through that. I don't wish it on anyone." I squeezed her, holding her tight.

"I haven't touched too much in your room yet. I figured you'd want to go through your stuff. I got the big stuff out of the way, but papers are thrown about."

"Thank you. I appreciate you cleaning what you have. I'm sorry again, Iris." I said, hugging her.

"It's not your fault, babe. Go change now, or we'll be late. You can clean up your room later." I nodded and headed up the stairs to change into my swimsuit.

I opened my bedroom door, and Iris was right. Papers were scattered around my room, many of them from the totes I had in my closet. Pictures of my friends and me at Sunset, which I had hung on my wall, were torn to shreds. "What was Jason looking for?"

I opened my dresser and quickly changed into my red and white lifeguard bikini. I slipped on black biker shorts over that and grabbed a hair tie from my nightstand.

Something on my bed caught my attention as I put my hair up. I bent down, running my hand over the sheet, and noticed holes in them. I pulled my sheet back and saw three slash marks on my mattress. "He had a knife?" My blood ran ice cold, and the air in my room felt thick.

Was he here to kill or scare me? Was he mad he couldn't find whatever he was looking for? I swallowed hard and quickly backed out of my room.

"You ready, Clo?" Iris shouted up the stairs.

"Yup, coming!" I rushed down the stairs, grabbed my flip-flops by the front door, and headed out to her Jeep.

My head was spinning with anxiety over what I discovered in my room. If I wanted Jason to stay away for good, I think now is the time to use the only dirt I have on the Hunt family. Jason's father has been cheating on his wife for three years with the assistant director of his company. Jason got drunk one night and cried to me about how he found them in his office when he went to visit him. He made Jason swear not to tell his mom, or he would disown him. In my email to his father, I will let him know that I know about his affair, and if he doesn't keep his son in check, I will tell his wife. It's the only real chance to keep me and my friends safe.

Iris pulled out of the driveway, blasting Blink-182 as I glanced at Ryder's house. He was watching out the window, and I smiled and waved. Iris pulled off, heading to the beach.

14

Clover

I made it to Sunset for my shift after a long day at the beach with Iris. She and I were on beach clean-up duty. We spent the entire day picking trash up on the beach, and I'm not complaining about that, but man, are my arms freaking sore!

I walked to the back room and opened my locker, where I found a work shirt to wear over my bikini top.

It was 80s night at Sunset tonight, so I pulled my makeup bag out of my locker and started rummaging through it. I threw my shirt on, took out my neon makeup palette, and walked to the mirror. I opened the palette and smeared the bright blue eyeshadow across my eyelid. I put the palette back and grabbed my little jar of sparkles, tapping some on my cheeks and brow bone. I threw my hair up in a side pony, separating some of my curls to give the frizzy 80s hair.

Satisfied with my makeup, I tied my shirt in a knot in the front and headed to the main bar. I walk through a crowd of people singing Beat It by Micheal Jackson. I felt my pocket buzzing, so I stepped to the side and pulled my phone out.

It was a text message from Ryder, "I miss you <3."

I blushed reading the text, my heart skipping several beats.

I stared at my phone, unsure of how to respond, when my Aunt came up to me, "I'm glad I caught you, Clover. I think you should head home. Jason is here, and he's been asking for you."

My mind started to race, and my fluttering heart quickly

turned to ice. "Thank you for telling me. Are you sure you don't need help tonight?"

My aunt shook her head, "He's been drinking, Clover. You need to go home. I'll have Uncle Rory kick him out." I nodded and quickly headed back to the back room.

I took out my phone and called Ryder. The phone rang twice before he picked up, "Clover? Are you okay?"

His immediate concern made my heart smile, "Hi! Yeah! My Aunt gave me the night off. We are overstaffed, and she's sending me home. I was wondering if you could pick me up?"

"Of course. I'll be right there." He said.

I breathed a sigh of relief. "Okay, thank you. I'll see you soon." I hung up the phone and placed it in my back pocket. I grabbed the baby wipes from my locker and started wiping off the blue eyeshadow and sparkles.

I threw the last wipe in the trash, looking over my face in the mirror when my eyes focused on something behind me.

I spun around and found Jason standing in the doorway. His expression was cold and distant. "Where you going, Clo? I thought you worked tonight."

"Home. Overstaffed." I replied, keeping it short and sweet.

Jason smirked, "Home? Our home? The one we bought together?"

I don't answer this time. Jason's looking for a fight, and I won't give him one.

Jason laughed, "You're giving me the silent treatment after you embarrassed me in front of my date the other night? I think you're forgetting your place, Clover." He stepped forward, closing the distance between us. "You're still a nobody."

Step.

"With nothing to your name."

Step.

"And no one to love you. Not even your parents."

He stood right in front of me now, and all I felt was the lasting sting of the punch he landed on my cheek over a year ago. "I may be a nobody. But at least I'm not a woman beater, unlike you."

Jason's cold expression turned dark, and I felt genuine fear for the first time in a long while.

My Uncle burst through the back room door and screamed at Jason, "Get the fuck out of my bar, and don't come back, Jason Hunt! You are banned from Sunset!"

Jason ignored my Uncle, giving me a smirk. He turned to my Uncle finally, and I let go of the breath I didn't know I was holding. "Whatever. Your bar is shitty anyway."

Jason left the room, and my Uncle rushed to me, asking if I was alright. "Yeah, I'm just shaken up. Thank you." I felt a buzzing in my back pocket and pulled my phone out to see a text from Ryder saying he was out front. "My friend is here to pick me up," I said.

I told my Uncle goodbye and headed out to the front, avoiding any looks I received on my way out.

15

Ryder

I pulled into Sunset's front parking lot and pulled out my phone to text Clover that I was there. Before I could hit send, a loud noise made me look up from my phone, and I saw Jason stumbling to his Jeep. He got into the driver's seat and took off, barely missing two parked cars. I hit send on the text and waited for Clover to come out.

A few moments later, Clover knocked on the passenger side window before entering my car. "Hi. Thank you again for picking me up."

"It's no problem. How are you? You look a little stressed?" It was written all over her face.

"I'm okay. Just tired. I had a *hectic* weekend." Her tone was playful, and I couldn't help but smile.

"The weekend doesn't have to stop. You can sleep at my place tonight if you'd like." I said as I backed out of the parking spot and began the drive back.

"I think I'll take you up on that. All my roommates are out tonight." She said.

"Oh? Where are they?" I asked, curious.

"Iris is a volunteer firefighter, and it's her week for the graveyard shift. Aiden also works the graveyard shift at the hospital. He's a nurse. And Rain is at the club across the bridge. She's an exotic dancer." Clover's smile was infectious as she spoke about her friends. She loved them.

When we arrived back at my house, Clover said she was

going to her house to get some clothes for the night. I stood at the end of her driveway, waiting for her, when I heard tires squeal on the street. On the corner, a Jeep sped off. It was too dark to see the driver, but whoever it was took off in a hurry.

Clover came out, locked her door behind her, and met me at the end of the driveway.

"What was that about?" Clover asked, looking in the direction where the Jeep sped off.

"I'm not sure. They were in a hurry, though." I said, and Clover laughed.

She held out her hand for me to take, and I laced my fingers with hers, pulling her face to mine with the other. She is so beautiful. I kissed her plump pink lips softly. Clover kissed me back, pressing herself into me. I pulled away, holding her face in the light of the street lamp that lights the end of her driveway, "I don't think I've ever met anyone like you, Clover."

"There's only one me, so of course you haven't." She said teasingly.

I howled with laughter, "We've got a comedian, I see."

"What? I was just stating the obvious!" She laughed.

I tugged her toward my house and said, "Come on, let's get you inside, Carrot Top."

She laughed as she followed me inside.

"There are three bedrooms you can choose from. They are all upstairs." I said, taking her overnight bag from her and leading her up the stairs.

"I thought I would be sleeping with you?" Clover questioned.

I halted, turning to her, "You can sleep with me if you'd like. I assumed you were tired from the weekend and wanted space."

Clover smiled shyly, "I would like to shower alone this time." I smiled, remembering our shower together. "But, if you don't mind, I would like to sleep with you?"

"Of course." I said, stroking her cheek, "Let me show you to the bathroom, and I'll put on a movie for us downstairs. Would you like popcorn?"

She smiled, "Yes, please."

◆ ◆ ◆

Thirty minutes later, I had the popcorn and an arrangement of snacks and picked a romantic comedy for us to watch. I dressed in my pajamas, which were just sweatpants, and I sat on the couch downstairs in front of the big TV, waiting for Clover. I heard the water shut off about five minutes ago, so she should be down soon.

"Hi," Clover said, entering the living room. She had on a silk pink two-piece short and tank top set. The fabric hung loose on her but clung to her shapely breasts.

I cleared my throat, "Hi. Sit with me? I have everything already here for us." I tapped the spot next to me, and Clover sat down and cuddled close. She laid her head on my bare chest, and I draped my arm around her as I turned on the movie.

"What movie are we watching?" She asked.

"Fools Rush In. A classic 90's rom-com." I admitted proudly.

"I love this movie!" Clover spun around to face me, "I wouldn't have pegged you as a guy who enjoys rom-coms."

"I'm a simple man. I don't hold any of those toxic masculinity values. I enjoy what I enjoy. No one can make me feel inferior because I enjoy rom-coms. The hierarchy that men put themselves on will be their downfall." Clover stared at me, mouth hanging open like I had just said something profound. "What?" I asked, genuinely curious.

"That was the hottest thing a man has ever said to me. I think that was the hottest thing any man has *ever* said, period." I laughed, but Clover still stared at me, her bottom lip tucked between her teeth. She looked me up and down, dangerously slow, placing her hand on my chest, "I think I want to skip the movie tonight." She said, leaning into me.

I gently caressed her face, "Then what do you want, Clover?"

In one swift move, Clover lifted her leg, straddling me. She lifted her silk shirt from her body, her soft skin begging to be touched. I reached my hand out, cupping her breast, and pinched her nipple between my thumb and forefinger. A delicious hum came from Clover, and she began to grind against me.

"Naughty girl, Clover." She laughed, thinking she had won this teasing game, but I don't like losing. I slid my hand from her breast up to her neck and quickly pulled her down to me, kissing her hard. I flipped her over onto the couch and ground my hard cock against her ass. She gasped, and I pulled back, slapping her ass, and she hummed with pleasure. "Be a good girl now." I pulled her shorts down, and Clover lifted her legs to help me remove them. "On your knees, but stay where you are." Clover did as I said and got on her knees on the couch. "Now, back to my question, what do you *want*, Clover?"

"I want you." She said.

I kissed her shoulder, "How do you want me, Clover?" I slipped a finger inside her dripping-wet pussy, making her mew.

"I–I–want, I–mmm–" I added a finger, and she blissfully growled, "I want to be on top." She said. I worked my fingers in and out, teasing her a little longer.

"As you wish." I nipped her shoulder, pulling my fingers out of her pussy and licking them clean. I lay on the couch's chaise and pulled my sweatpants off when Clover stopped me.

"Allow me," She pulled my pants down and held my cock in her hands. She began to stroke me up and down. My head fell back when she dragged her tongue over the tip, swirling it around. She works my cock in her mouth while her hands assist her.

"Fuck, Clover." I moaned, reaching down to gather her hair in my hands, and she let out a low hum. She worked my cock, tip to base, and it wasn't long before I was on the edge. I gripped her hair, pulling her from my cock as I sat up and kissed her. I let go of her hair, and she stood, lifting my chin to look at her. Clover moved slowly, straddling me and lowering herself to my lap. She placed a hand on my chest and pushed me back down on the couch. My cock rubbed against her entrance, and Clover let out a low hum once again. She traced her fingers lightly around my chest down to my stomach. Her eyes met mine as she lowered herself onto my cock, letting out a soft moan.

"Ryder," She breathed, and I let her take over. She was slow at first, but she picked up her pace, placing her hands against my chest for leverage. I grabbed onto her hips, pushing myself deeper into her, and she let out a moan. Clover batted my hands away and repositioned herself with her feet on the edge of the chaise, and now it was my turn to let out a moan as Clover lowered herself once again. My cock was buried deep inside her as she bounced up and down. She worked herself up, and her orgasm was so close her pussy had a vice grip on my cock. I sat up, grabbing her hips to hold her steady, and Clover draped her arms around my shoulder as I began to rock her back and forth.

"Oh, yes! Right there, Ryder!" Clover shouted, threading her hands through my hair. "I'm going to come!"

I smirked, pushing her harder, "Come for me, Clover." She yelped, her pussy squeezing my cock, "Come for me, baby." Clover held my gaze as she came undone around my cock, her orgasm pushing me over the edge, and we came together.

We collapsed onto the couch, and I scooped her into my arms, holding her close. "So that's what you wanted," I said, making Clover laugh as I kissed her soft skin anywhere I could.

"If you keep kissing me like that, I will want it again." She playfully warned.

"We have all night, Clover." I rebuttled and continued my trail of kisses.

A low hum comes from her lips, and I know I've won. I took her nipple into my mouth, and she hissed. "You are insatiable, Ryder Reed." She said as I moved to hover over her.

"And you like it, Clover Langley."

16

Clover

I rolled over in bed, stretching awake. My eyes opened to see Ryder sleeping soundly. An image I've grown used to seeing is that I've spent every night for a week and a half here with him since that night at Sunset. I still had to go to work and see my roommates, but I always returned to him.

I quietly got up and started my morning routine. I entered the shower and let the steamy water massage my skin.

The morning after I spent the first night here, I sent Jason's father the email detailing his son's break-in and my knowledge of his affair, and I haven't seen or heard from Jason since. I hope it was enough to have his father talk some sense into him or at least send him away again. But I can't shake the feeling that he's just waiting.

He has always been vindictive, and I'm sure that part of him hasn't changed with one talk with his father. I made a deal with his father not to involve the cops, but only if he paid the house on C Street off, signed it over to me, and kept Jason away from me. I had all the proof I needed to put him in jail. Iris helped me put it together while staying with her after I left Jason. And just like that, his father shipped him off to rehab and handed the keys to the house over to me a week later.

I turned the shower off, wrapped a towel around myself, and headed to the closet to find my bag of clothes. My anxiety this past week has been through the roof as I waited for the other foot to drop and for Jason to do something drastic, but today, I wasn't going to let it affect me. It's been over a week, and I can't let it control me.

Ryder has a surprise planned for us today, and I have today off because it's the Fourth of July. I wouldn't let my worries sour my time with him. I put on one of my comfy nightgowns and returned to the bathroom. I approached the sink and began to brush my hair. The mirror was still fogged from my shower, so I swiped a dry washcloth across it and saw Ryder standing behind me.

I yelped, turning to swat him away for scaring me, "Ryder! Don't scare me like that!"

He laughed, scooping me into his arms and setting me down on the counter next to the sink. "Good morning." He said, angling my face up towards him. He kissed my lips softly, and I don't think the butterfly feeling will ever disappear. Ryder's soft and gentle in a way that makes me crave his presence.

"Good morning. Are you ready to tell me about the surprise?" I cocked my eyebrow, letting him know I wasn't going to give in to his charm.

"That would ruin the surprise. You will find out after breakfast." He grabbed his toothbrush and began to brush his teeth. "Go eat breakfast, Clover. You'll find out quicker," he said in between brushing.

I rolled my eyes, "Fine." I hopped off the counter and went downstairs.

◆ ◆ ◆

Ryder told me to dress in beach attire, so I chose a slinky black bikini to drive him crazy, just like he drives me crazy with surprises.

We pulled up to Flag Ponds Beach, and the surprise was worth it. I haven't been here in so long, but it's my favorite beach in Calvert County. The beach is shelly, and it's known for being a hub for shark teeth. I found one here the last time I came. I was with my parents before things got bad, and I remember my dad being so proud of me.

The memory stung a little, but it was one of the good ones.

"I love this beach. I haven't been here in forever." I said to Ryder as we pulled into the park. We pull up next to a silver Jeep that looks like Iris's.

"Some scary lady told me it was," Ryder said, looking out the rearview. I looked out the passenger rearview and saw Iris, Rain, and Aiden standing at the back of her Jeep with beach chairs and bags.

"You invited my friends?" I asked, bewildered.

"They invited themselves, but I said it was a good idea. You needed a beach day, and what better day than the Fourth of July and getting to spend it with the people who matter most to you?"

I smiled, "Thank you." I said softly, trying not to cry.

"Let's get you on the beach!" He said, putting his sunglasses on.

We exited the car, gathered our beach bags, and started the hike to the beach. Aiden and Ryder talked to each other on the way there because Iris and Rain had kidnapped me to talk about Ryder.

"You have to tell us what's been going on." Rain said.

"Yeah. You've been practically living there, and sometimes I forget you live with us!" Iris said a little too loud.

"Shh! Listen, I didn't think I would be there every night either, but there's something utterly magnetic about Ryder," I admitted. "I can't seem to keep away."

Rain snickered, "You can't seem to get off of him either."

Iris laughed, and I playfully jabbed Rain.

"You wouldn't either if you knew what kind of lover he is. He's *very* giving." I teased. Iris gagged, and Rain giggled. "He's also a very kind and gentle person. Someone completely different from anyone I've ever dated. And he makes me happy."

"We are happy for you, Clover," Iris said, smiling at me.

"As long as you're happy, we are happy." Rain said in agreement.

"I'm the happiest I've been in a long time." It's the truth.

Every moment with Ryder excited me, and I dreaded being apart from him.

Aiden came up behind us, taking Iris and Rain by the hands and pulling them into a dance. He loudly sang Gimmie More by Britney Spears, and Iris and Rain chimed in, dancing a few yards away. Ryder wrapped his arms around my shoulders and kissed the top of my head.

"I like your friends." He said.

"You just met them." I teased, but on the inside, I was gleaming.

Jason did his best to isolate me from them the last couple of months we were together. He never wanted me to hang out with them, so hearing that Ryder likes them felt like a weight was lifted off my shoulders.

"I do. I think your friends all have exciting lives and that you all peacefully coexist under one roof. You have your own support village, and honestly, it's refreshing to see." Ryder said.

Knowing Ryder's past, my heart broke for him. It's one thing to come to terms with being adopted, which is still very hard, but I can't imagine what it's like to age out of the system. He never had a support system until he was a teenager. I wouldn't be as kind and gentle if it were me. I admire him more now that I've spent more time with him. He told me stories about the horrible things he's witnessed or things Ryder had done himself that he's not proud of, and I can't blame him for any of it. He was just a kid trying to survive.

I angled my head towards him, "I think they like you, too." Ryder kissed my brow.

We caught up with my friends and headed to the beach.

◆ ◆ ◆

We spent most of the afternoon in the water, playing chicken and searching for shells and shark teeth. When we started packing up, Ryder walked over to a beach vendor to grab water bottles for all of us for the ride home.

Aiden cleared his throat, "So, Clo, when's the wedding?"

I laughed, but Aiden just smiled.

"What?" I asked.

Iris and Rain both laughed, coming up behind us.

"You're totally in Love, Clover. With a capital L," Iris said.

"And so is he." Rain pointed out.

I chose to stay silent because I knew the truth, as did they. I don't know how to say it out loud or if I should.

"He's a great guy, Clo," Rain said. "We see how he looks at you. He adores you." Iris and Aiden nodded in agreement. "Does he have a brother by chance?" Rain added.

I shook my head, laughing, "No, he doesn't."

Rain sucked her teeth, and it made me laugh again.

"We just wanted to tell you that we approve. Ryder is lovely, and we will support you wherever you take your relationship." Aiden chimed, and Iris and Rain nodded.

"Thank you. I love you guys," I said, motioning them to bring in a group hug. They squished me with their love as Ryder returned with the water.

He handed each of us one, and we started the journey back to the cars.

◆ ◆ ◆

Ryder drove us back to his place, but he said it was only to shower and change because we were going to my house to watch the fireworks. Ryder gave me the upstairs bathroom, and I did my business quickly, excited for the night to start.

Ryder exited the downstairs bathroom as I came down the stairs. "Can we stop at the liquor store and grab something before we head over?" I asked. "I think I want to get a little drunk tonight."

Ryder kissed me at the bottom of the steps. "There's already some chilling in the fridge."

I walked over to the fridge and opened it to find my top three faves, "But how did—Iris."

Of course, Iris was involved in this. I laughed, closing the fridge.

"I'll be ready to go in a few minutes. Can you put the alcohol in the bags I left on the counter?" Ryder asked.

"Of course." I smiled.

He turned, heading up the stairs, and I found the bags and began to put the alcohol in them.

Ryder joined me moments later, grabbing the bags as we made our way over to my house. I opened the door, and Aiden greeted us, taking a bag from Ryder and showing him to our kitchen.

I joined Rain and Iris on the couch, and it seemed Rain had Iris in a makeup vice grip, spreading red, blue, and silver glitter on her cheekbones.

"Just sit still, Iz! You aren't going to die from glitter!" Rain shouted.

"It's the herpes of the craft world! You've infected me with craft herpes! Are you happy?" Iris shouted back.

"Very! You look so cute now, you little blonde-haired goblin!" Rain turned to me, "Oh, good, your turn!" She said, already coming at me with a finger full of glitter. She dabbed it around on my cheekbones as I sat still, waiting for Rain to be satisfied. "See, Iris, was it that hard?" Iris made a face at her behind her back as Rain moved to the kitchen.

Ryder sat next to me, handing me one of my drinks. "Thank you," I said, taking a sip.

"No problem. So, Iris, what games are we playing?" Ryder asked.

I turned my attention to Iris, and she jumped up and headed for the game shelf we kept in our living room. "We will play charades, and then, if we have time, Cards Against Humanity. Keep it classy, you know?" Iris said, pulling down the basket of our handmade charade cards. "Winners take a shot, and losers take three." She added.

Aiden and Rain made their way to the couch from the kitchen and watched as Iris went first. She started to make gestures to have us guess who she was, but I couldn't help but take a step back and look around at the people in my life.

I thought after my parents died that I wouldn't find a family again, but I couldn't have been more wrong. Ryder being here confirmed what I already knew deep down.

I love him.

17

Ryder

I stared at the papers before me, the lines and words blurring. I pinched the bridge of my nose, shut my eyes, and took a deep breath.

Blueprints and a map of the town of Solomons were laid on my home office desk.

The potential sales I contacted haven't returned my calls, so I'm looking into businesses on the strip that are in financial hardship and would be looking to sell quickly. I've been here for four weeks already, and my boss is growing restless because I haven't made any headway on the project. I've been spending all my time with Clover since I got to Solomons instead.

During the last several weeks, we've spent every moment we could with each other until this weekend. Clover is spending it with her friends at her place, and I encouraged her to do so. I needed to catch up on work, and she needed to catch up with her girlfriends.

I ran my hands through my hair, looking over all the businesses, when a familiar name appeared on my screen.

Sunset Escape.

Clover's Uncle has had some loan issues, and the bank might be foreclosing on them in the future. The thought of Clover being devastated if she found this out crossed my mind, and a knot formed deep in my stomach.

After I find a place to put the strip mall, I can ask David to help out the bar. He praised the bar so highly that I'm sure he'd be interested in making a deal.

I printed out what was on my screen, put it in my work folder, and got back to work.

◆ ◆ ◆

I pulled into LookOut's parking lot and walked inside to grab my to-go order. The hostess smiled at me, and I told her my order number for pick-up. They let me know it would be a few minutes. I nodded, walked back to the waiting area, and took out my phone to text Clover when I saw Jason across the restaurant at the bar.

"Fuck," I said under my breath as I made eye contact with him. I could see him coming this way out of the corner of my eye, and I hoped he'd just pass me by.

"Hey!" He said obnoxiously loud, drawing attention to himself. "I'm Jason Hunt. Nice to meet you." He stuck his hand out for a handshake, but I stared him down. "Oh, so that's how you wanna be, okay? I get it. You're seeing Clover, and she's probably told you all about us."

Again, I won't dignify him with an answer, but whatever past they had together is none of my business.

"We were engaged, you see, but she got cold feet and called it off. She has commitment issues." He pauses, leaning in to whisper, "And once she finds out why you're here, she'll leave you too."

I said nothing and watched him walk past me and out the door.

The hostess brought out my order, and I thanked her and returned to my car. I looked around to see if Jason was hanging around, but no one was in the parking lot. I got in my car, and Jason's words haunted me. Clover loves it here, but would she end what we have over it? I don't want to lose the career I've built over the last decade, and I don't want to lose Clover, either.

There has to be a way for me to keep both.

I will find a way.

18

Clover

It's Two Dollar Tuesdays at Sunset today, and my shift started an hour ago. The summer crowds are dying down since it's the first week of August, and the lack of a crowd has left me to my anxieties, and recently, there's a lot of them.

Ryder has been distant for the last two weeks. He's still kind and gentle like he was, but he's just distant. Since I returned from the girl's weekend, he's been more reclusive and spends much of his free time in his office. He said it's because he has a lot of work to catch up on, but my intuition tells me it's something else. I don't know what 'else' is, but I hoped he wasn't cheating on me.

Not knowing what it is is driving me up a wall. I racked my brain for something I'd done or said that might be the reason for Ryder's distance, but I couldn't think of anything.

I'm scared I'm losing him, but I will confront him tomorrow on my day off. I will sleep at my house tonight and go over first thing. If he has another woman over, she'll still be there.

My heart broke thinking of him with another woman, but there's no other explanation for his distancing.

I hoped.

◆ ◆ ◆

I woke up bright and early the next day, hoping to catch Ryder. But when I looked out the window, I saw his car missing from the driveway. I decided to go over anyway and wait for him to get back.

We needed a conversion either way, whether he wanted to or not.

I entered his house and called for Ryder, but there was no answer. My intuition was telling me to go upstairs, so I did. My heart was pounding in my ears as I gripped the main bedroom knob, turned it, and peered into the room.

Empty.

I breathed a sigh of relief and continued my search into his office. I pushed open the door, and in the room was a large table in the middle and an L-shaped desk in the far back corner. I've never been in this room before, but I see Ryder's work scattered all over the table.

I walked up to the table and saw blueprints for Solomons and blueprints for properties on the island. I stared at them, confused, but kept searching. I picked up a black folder off the end of the table and started looking through it. My heart dropped seeing my Uncle's bar on a list for potential sale. I looked through the folder and found a mock blueprint of a strip mall.

Suddenly, it all clicked.

Ryder told me his job but never told me what he was doing in Solomons. Did he sleep with me in hopes I would have my Uncle sell him his bar? The cherry on top of a business deal?

I felt sick.

"Clover, I can explain," Ryder said from the doorway.

"Explain what, Ryder? I'm just a stepping stone for you to get to my Uncle. You know, I thought you were cheating on me, but how silly of me to think that because we aren't even together, and we never were." I threw the folder down and pushed my way past him.

"Clover, please, wait!" Ryder shouted behind me.

"No! You've pushed me away for two weeks, Ryder. You don't get to explain now." I opened the front door, looking back once more as tears flooded my cheeks, "Goodbye, Ryder Reed." I slammed the door, leaving a piece of me behind.

19

Clover

It's been three days since I've seen Ryder. My anger towards him has been replaced by sadness. Sadness for how I reacted, sadness for how he didn't tell me the truth, and sadness for what we could have been. I saw myself marrying Ryder, and now I don't know what I want.

I've called out of work every day since our fight, and I've ignored all his texts and calls because I don't want to face the truth. I'm scared I've overreacted and that he wants nothing to do with me now, but seeing my Uncle's name on the list for potential sales sent me over the edge.

Maybe after the weekend, I'll give him a chance to explain, and perhaps he'll give me a chance to apologize.

Iris and Rain have been with me the last few days, letting me cry on their shoulders. They have been my voice of reason and pointed out that I didn't let Ryder explain before I blew up at him. They reassured me that I was valid in my feelings, but how I reacted was wrong.

Tonight is my first night alone since the fight. Iris and Rain had to return to work, and Aiden was always on the graveyard shift.

I ordered Chinese food for dinner tonight, and the delivery driver should be here any minute. I changed into fresh pajamas and bolted down the steps when I heard the doorbell ring.

The delivery boy handed me my food, and I tipped him. But before I closed the door, I caught Ryder standing at the end of his driveway, looking over at me. I locked eyes with him, and I swallowed hard.

Everything was still fresh, and my anger bubbled under my skin. Ryder stepped toward my house, and I slammed my front door shut and walked into my kitchen. Tears threatened to fall, but I kept it together. I wasn't going to cry tonight. I threw my phone on the kitchen counter and angrily plated my Chinese food.

I took my plate and moved to the living room, scooping up the remote and turning on one of my Sad Girl movies. I searched through the titles and found Twilight, one of my favorites.

I will sit here all weekend and watch movies where the lead female gets her heart broken over an overrated, beautiful, sexy man. Because the other option is to face reality, and I can't even step out of my front door.

The movie started, and I shoveled my food into my mouth, hoping it would make me feel better soon.

I jolted awake, hearing glass shatter. At first, I assumed it was the movie playing, but when I looked at the TV screen, it was black. The movie was over, so the sound must have come from inside.

Reality hit me.

Someone was breaking into my house.

I look around the room and see no one. I quietly got off the couch and quickly made it to the steps.

The glass shattering sounded like it came from downstairs, so I needed to go up.

I reached my bedroom and frantically searched for my phone to call the police. "Where the fuck is it?" I whispered to myself. I checked my pockets and the charger beside my bed, but it wasn't there. I think back to tonight, and I remember I put it on the kitchen counter earlier after I saw Ryder outside. "Fuck."

I opened my bedroom door slowly, praying it didn't make a

sound. I crawled on my hands and knees down the hallway and steps.

The house was silent, and I thought maybe I dreamt of the sound, but my intuition told me otherwise. I saw my phone on the counter, and I slowly made my way over, grabbed it, and frantically tried to unlock it.

The screen unlocked, and I opened the phone app to dial the number when a hand covered my mouth, and my vision went dark.

20

Ryder

I watched Clover pay for her takeout, and I wanted nothing more than to go over there and tell her how sorry I was. I made a terrible mistake and wanted to prove that she meant more to me than anything else. I didn't want to lose the woman I love. But the moment Clover saw me, she slammed the door just like she did on the day she left.

A few hours have passed since then, and I've done nothing but stew on everything.

I wasn't going to wait for Clover to come to me. She needed to hear the truth. She deserved that much. I would gather myself and march my sorry ass over to Clover's house.

I opened my front door and heard the faintest sound of glass breaking. The noise sent a chill down my spine. I held my phone in my hand as I slowly approached, dialing the number for 911. I knew something was wrong and confirmed that when I heard the worst sound on Earth.

Clover's scream pierced through my soul like a steel blade.

21

Clover

I come to in my kitchen with a gag in my mouth and my hands tied behind my back. I tugged on my restraints and could feel that they weren't tight enough. I could wiggle my hands out of them, but I needed to be smart and not draw attention to myself.

I picked my head up to look around the room and saw Jason sitting across from me. My heart fell to the pit of my stomach as I saw the evil look in his eye from the night he cornered me at Sunsets.

I don't pray, but in this moment, I did.

Jason was here to kill me because I hurt his ego or something worse.

"Hello, Clover. Thought you got rid of me, huh?" I stared at him, trying not to let off my fear. "Where's your boyfriend, huh? Oh, that's right, you broke up with him because you found out the truth. I warned him you would. And it looks like I was right." I worked my hands slowly back and forth, loosening the knots. Jason stood, and I paused my escape as he came over, gripping me by my hair and whispering in my ear, "If you scream, I'll gut you right here." He pulled the gag from my mouth and leaned against the counter.

"What do you want from me, Jason?" I asked. I needed to keep him talking if I didn't want him to notice I was trying to escape.

"Simple. You will marry me." I laughed in his face, and Jason sneered.

"You think I'll marry you?"

I was in utter disbelief. He was insane.

"I don't think you have a choice. The little email you sent my father got me disowned. So I started digging and discovered that your Uncle is in financial trouble with the bank. He owes a pretty penny, and if he doesn't have it figured out by Christmas, Sunset Escape will be no more. And your family will be in ruins. But—not if you marry me and convince Uncle Rory to sign it over to you, and then you'll give it to me."

"My Uncle will never agree to this, Jason. This is a ridiculous plan!" I watched as he loomed over me, and I felt helpless. Jason flashed a knife, dragging it across my face.

"You will do this, or I'll kill that prick across the street." my body went still, "You love him, don't you?" I didn't answer. "I always knew you were a fucking whore. Fucking the guy who wants to build a strip mall on the island. Do you know what everyone will say once they find out? You'll be more hated than me." Jason laughed.

"What if I can't get my Uncle to sell me Sunset? What then, Jason?" My hands were almost free, but I just needed to buy myself more time. Jason dragged the knife down to the strap of my pajama top and cut the strap. I gasped as he ran the cold blade over my chest, pushing the fabric of my top down to reveal my breast.

"Then I guess you better get used to the streets of D.C. You made me lose my inheritance, Clover. I need that money and will sell you to anyone who can pay the price. Get your Uncle to give you the bar, and we won't have to resort to such measures." He smiled wickedly, and I swallowed hard. Jason dragged his attention back down to my breast.

The sick fuck is getting off on this.

My hand came loose, and as Jason stared at my breast, he didn't see me pull my head back before I slammed it into his face. I heard the crunch of bone, and Jason fell back onto the floor. I stumbled, got up, and bolted for the front door. I was almost there until a hand gripped me by my hair and ripped me backward. I screamed as I fell to the ground, but I quickly got to my feet and tried to run for the stairs. But Jason was quicker. He gripped me by my hair again and pinned me to the kitchen island.

Jason held the knife to my throat, and I pleaded with him not to do it. "Please, Jason! I'm sorry!"

"Shut up, bitch!" He shouted, making me cry harder.

This was it.

He was going to kill me.

I was going to die in the house where he first put his hands on me. Poetic irony.

I heard a banging from the front door, followed by a loud boom. Ryder stormed into the kitchen, and Jason picked me up, using me as a shield between them.

Ryder gave Jason a death glare as he taunted him with me. "I was wondering when he'd show up," Jason said into my ear.

"Let her go, and you can walk away," Ryder warned.

"And what? Let go of my pretty little cash cow? I don't think so." Jason bit back. He dug the knife into my skin, and I cried out.

"Enough, Jason!" Ryder shouted. I looked into Ryder's eyes and saw he was just as scared as I was.

"Aww, how touching. But if you'll excuse us, we have a flight to Vegas to catch." My heart leaped in my throat as Jason began to drag me away. "If you follow us, she dies," Jason told Ryder.

Ryder reluctantly stayed put as Jason dragged me out the front door onto the lawn.

Suddenly, flood lights surrounded us, and a voice shouted over a loudspeaker that it was the sheriff's department. "We have you surrounded! Let go of the girl, and drop your weapon!"

"No. No, no, no, no!!" Jason shouted, throwing me to the ground. I quickly got up and ran right into Ryder's arms. He hugged me tight and asked me if I was okay. I nodded as Ryder wiped my tears away.

Jason was put into handcuffs by three police officers and loaded into the back of a police cruiser. Ryder shook hands with a cop and thanked them for showing up as quickly as they did. He told Ryder they needed me for questioning, but it could wait until morning. Ryder nodded, and he tried to take me back into my house.

"No! I'm never stepping foot into this house again. Please take me back to your house, Ryder, please." I begged.

"Shhh. Shhh. Of course, Clover. Come on, let's get you home."

◆ ◆ ◆

Several days have passed since the incident with Jason. I've moved in with Ryder again because I still can't be in the house. We haven't discussed what happened between us, and I'm unsure if I want to. I'm not ready to have my heart broken again, but Ryder asked me to dinner tonight, and I owe him that much.

I picked out a short green sundress I had in my overnight bag and put it on. I put a little mascara and a touch of lip gloss on in the bathroom mirror to finish the look and headed downstairs. Ryder was at the bottom steps waiting for me, and I couldn't help but smile seeing him in a suit again.

"Ready for dinner?" He asked, holding out his arm for me to take.

"Yes," I said with a smile, but inside I panicked.

The drive to the restaurant was quick. It was the Tap House Grille on the other side of the bay. We were seated quickly, and I felt my heart rate rise every second he stared at me.

"Before we order, I want to tell you something," Ryder admitted.

Here we go. I swallowed hard and prepared myself for the worst.

"I was wrong to keep you in the dark about why I was here. I should have told you." Ryder paused, and I was on the edge of my seat. "I spent the last two weeks figuring out a way not to build here. I found an environmental law that states islands under three square miles cannot have industrial buildings, only residential ones. I've already told my boss, and he's canceled the project."

I gasped and soon felt the tears welling up, "Thank you, Ryder."

"There's more," he said, placing a piece of paper on the table and sliding it over to me. I picked it up and gasped, "Your uncle's loan has been paid off in full. I told my boss about the bar, and he was more than willing to help. He was the one who recommended I go to Sunset the night I meet you." Ryder said. I stared at the banknote, the big red letters spelled paid, and tears threatened to fall.

"That's not all," Ryder said, getting up and then down on one knee. My hand flew over my mouth, and the happy tears spilled over. "Clover Langley, I love you more than life itself. I don't want to live in a world without you in it. Would you do me the honor of becoming my wife?"

I stared at the gorgeous Topaz and Opal ring. The stones were set in a setting that reminded me of something you'd find in Lord of the Rings. It was perfectly me. "Yes, Ryder Reed. I will marry you. I love you, too." Ryder scooped me into an embrace and kissed me hard.

"I told you I'd get you to say 'I do' again," Ryder said, pulling me in for another kiss, and I let him, savoring this moment forever.

EPILOGUE

Clover

Today was the first day of spring, which meant Ryder would be coming home in a few days. He spent the winter traveling to make up for losing this project, but soon, he wouldn't have to travel anymore.

Ryder was promoted at work, meaning he no longer had to travel. We bought the house Ryder was staying in.

It just happened to go on the market the day Ryder was leaving, and he pulled some strings and ended up getting the house.

I've spent the winter decorating our new home and planning our summer wedding with my maid of honor, Iris. She was coming over today to help me finalize the seating chart for the reception.

The doorbell rang, and I skipped over to answer it.

"Are you ready for seating arrangements?" Iris asked in an over-enthusiastic tone.

"Ready to get it over with." I rebuttled.

Iris scoffed, "You and I, both, sister." I watched as Iris put down the binder of all the wedding details on the kitchen table. Her face was red and flushed like she had been crying.

"Are you okay, Iz?" I asked.

"What? Oh, yeah, I'm fine." Iris waved her hand dismissively.

"Are you sure you look, I don't know, not your usual self?"

"Yes, I'm fine. Now, about the seating," Iris started going on about who should sit where and why, and I let her take control. She paired family and friends first, saving the tables for the bridesmaids and groomsmen last.

"You didn't leave room for plus-ones for the bridesmaids or groomsmen," I interjected.

Iris laughed, "And who would we bring?"

She may be laughing, but her words had a bit of a bite. "I don't know. Do you have someone in mind?" Iris scoffed, but a knock on my front door stopped her before she could answer. "We aren't finished with this conversion," I tell her and go to answer my front door.

I answered the door, and a huge bouquet greeted me.

Out from behind, Ryder stood, smiling. I screamed and jumped into his arms, knocking the flowers to the ground. "I'm happy to see you too, love." He kissed me, and I told him I was busy with Iris in the kitchen doing wedding planning. He got the hint and headed up the stairs to unpack his suitcase. I walked back into the kitchen and saw Iris had cleaned up.

"But what about the plus-ones?" I asked, and Iris glared at me. I threw my hands up, "Okay. Fine. We will do this another day."

"You don't understand how lucky you are, Clover," Iris said.

"What?" I asked, surprised by her tone.

"You get to be open and free, while some of us don't have that luxury." She bit.

"Iris, what is this about? This attitude isn't about my stupid seating chart, and I don't appreciate the way you're speaking to me." I warned.

"Whatever. You wouldn't understand." Iris said, pushing past me.

"Iris!" I called for her, but she ran out the door like a bat of hell.

Something was definitely going on with Iris, and she was lashing out. Her words hurt, but I know she didn't mean it. I'll talk with her later, but I need to see my man for now.

Ryder came down the stairs and asked if I was okay. I threw

my arms around his neck and pulled him into a kiss. "I'm fine. It's nothing. Iris being Iris." I kissed him again, "But what's not nothing is how incredibly horny I am right now."

"Oh really?" he said between kisses, "I think I can help with that."

"Mmm, I think I would like that." I hummed.

Ryder kissed his way down my neck, pulling the straps of my dress down. I threw my head back, threading my fingers through his hair as he pulled us to the living room. Ryder kissed his way back up my neck and guided me down to the couch. He ran his hands up my thigh and pulled my panties off, and slipped two fingers into my pussy.

"Ryder!" I gasped. He smiled against my lips and began pumping his fingers in and out. I held his face to mine, making him look me in the eyes as he fingered me. "I've missed you," I whispered.

Ryder picked up his pace, "I've missed you so much, baby. I couldn't get back here fast enough." He worked his fingers faster, "Every night I laid to sleep, it was a constant reminder that I was one night closer to you." I was bucking against his hand, my orgasm so close. I held on to his gaze, looking deep into those brown eyes. "One night closer to kissing you. One night closer to being buried so deep inside you I make you forget I was gone in the first place."

"Fuck!" I come hard around Ryder's fingers, my legs shaking in pure ecstasy. I let go of Ryder, falling back onto the couch, panting. "Holy shit. Maybe you did miss me."

Ryder laughed, pulling me under him. "I missed you terribly. I'm happy to be home." He kissed me softly as I began to unbutton his shirt. Ryder made no delay, sitting up to remove his clothes, and I slipped my dress off.

Ryder climbed on top of me again, grabbing my breasts in both his hands and sucking one of my nipples in his mouth as he pinched the other. I hummed, catching my bottom lip between my teeth. His cock teased my entrance, and I wiggled my hips down to rub my clit against him. Ryder moaned as he swirled his tongue around my nipple, driving me insane.

Ryder chuckled, popping my breast out of his mouth, sitting up and grabbing his cock. "So impatient." He rubbed the tip of his cock up and down on my clit. "God, you're so fucking wet, Clover. I could slip right in." He pushed the tip of his cock into me but pulled it out, teasing me. I growled, making Ryder laugh. "You want me to fuck you, baby?"

"Yes, Ryder. Please. Please fuck me." I mewed. Ryder leaned forward, his cock still teasing my entrance, as he gripped my neck and kissed me hard, driving his cock into me. "Ryder!" I gasped as he thrust inside me fervently, my orgasm building quickly.

"Is my pretty little wife going to come around my cock?" He said into my ear.

"Yes," I said, barely holding on to my reality.

"Come for me, Clover."

And like a command, I came so hard that I swore I saw stars. Ryder was about to pull out of me when I locked my legs around his waist, "Come inside me, Ryder. fill me up, please!" Ryder thrusts picked up, and soon, he came filling me up as promised. He collapsed on the couch next to me and embraced me.

"How's that for a homecoming?" I said, giggling.

"Couldn't have asked for a better one. The only thing I needed was the woman I love." Ryder nestled his head to mine, "I love you."

I smiled, "I love you too."

END

ACKNOWLEDGMENTS

Thank you so much for reading Loving! This was such a fun book to write, and I can't wait to work on the second book, Embracing–Solomons Island, which follows Iris!

You can follow me on all my socials here → https://linktr.ee/AuthorCABurkhart

Check out my Fantasy romance series Kingdom of Rinnia-Awakened Uner the Blood Moon here → https://www.amazon.com/dp/B0CTR4H62C?ref_=pe_93986420_775043100

Made in the USA
Middletown, DE
05 September 2024

59849519R00060